The Three-Berry Academy

Also by Joseph Helgerson

Horns & Wrinkles
Crows & Cards
The Lost Galumpus

You can reach Joseph Helgerson at:

joe@josephhelgerson.com

The Three-Berry Academy

Blue Wing Shorts: Book 1

Joseph Helgerson

Illustrations by Lauren Mortimer

Deepthink Books

Text copyright © 2024 by Joseph Helgerson
Illustrations copyright © by Lauren Mortimer
Cover art copyright © 2024 by Jenny Zemanek
All rights reserved.

Deepthink Books
Minneapolis MN

The text of this book is set in Garamond.

Library of Congress Control Number: 2024906524
Helgerson, Joseph
The Three-Berry Academy by Joseph Helgerson
Illustrations by Lauren Mortimer

ISBN 978-1-949615-01-2 (laminate hardcover)
ISBN 978-1-949615-04-3 (duskjacket hardcover)
ISBN 978-1-949615-03-6 (paperback)
ISBN 978-1-949615-02-9 (e-book)

Summary: A magical stretch of the Mississippi River near Blue Wing, Minnesota, is home to a one-room schoolhouse for river trolls. The headmistress of that school, Ms. Quiet Quickthorn, must catch her students at the start of every school year.

[1. Fantasy--Fiction. 2. Trolls--Fiction. 3. Middle-grade--Fiction. 4. Mississippi River--Fiction. 5. Elementary School--Fiction. 6. Humor--Fiction.]

Printed in the United States

For Maggie

Contents

Quiet Quickthorn	1
Yes Gartooth	4
Tenpenny Hammertoe	15
Blaze Wrinklesnout	18
Two Shellcruncher	26
Nod Logrot	38
Mudd Dimwater	45
Boom Halfsnout	52
Kazoo Ripp	62
Gravy Drop-off	66
Smuch Lipsmacker	77
Happy Mudneck	83
First-grade Dripple	88
One-Bite Skeeterfog	100
Burpetta Sludge	102
Nor-I Brighteye	111
The Old Man	113
Dimwhittle Wetwater	118
Steamalita Willowbug	123
Arithmetic Icksome	139
Nibble Nettleburst	143
Iffy Fishfly	146
Precocious Grabsome	161
Wabash Smoothwater	166
Booky Doublemuck	178
Collection Day	191
The Bell	204

The Three-Berry Academy

Quiet Quickthorn

I'm not about to say how long I've been the headmistress at the Three-Berry Academy for the Totally Gifted. A teacher is entitled to some secrets.

But I will say that my school sits at the bottom of Big Mouth Slough. That's near the small town of Blue Wing on the Mississippi. We meet in a one-room schoolhouse that once overlooked Yellow Cat Bottoms. Upstream, I'm talking. The flood of '52 ended that deal. High waters swept the building off its foundation, carrying it downstream until two mighty cottonwoods caught and sank it in front of a riverbank covered with wild berries.

Other facts about the Three-Berry Academy: For uniforms, my students wear oversized football jerseys that are purple with gold trim. Quite handsome.

Enrollment varies from year to year, but I generally round up twenty to thirty students a year.

Of course classes are held only at night. This is a proper school.

I have posted a hefty reward for any information leading to the return of the school's bell!

I teach grades one through eight. Subjects include:

Minnow Herding
Beginning, Middle, and Advanced River Smells
Basic Fishnet Escape
Salvage Ethics
Mud Daubing
Story Stretching
River Troll Lore
Rock Troll Myths
Eggs and Grubs to Avoid
Daylight Survival
Introduction to River Charms
Heron Wading
Eel Avoidance
Riverograph

Arithmetic and counting are touched upon.

Strict discipline is maintained with the help of several snapping turtles who have no sense of humor and little sense of smell.

If you're still not convinced, check around. Everyone will tell you that Quiet Quickthorn (that's me) is well known in the district for the way my left eye wanders and my guarantee that everyone graduates.

If someone doesn't earn a diploma while alive, then he or she has to finish up once dead. The school contract requires it, and no one has ever doubted that I have sufficient grit to teach a ghost. There's enough steel in my voice to build a bridge. And I've been told that the way I snap questions brings to mind a bullwhip. Oh yes, students leap out of their chairs when I call upon them. Classroom discussions are so lively there's often no need for recess. More time for studies, I say.

And here's one last thing to think about—in order to attend the Three-Berry you must be a river troll. I certainly am.

Yes Gartooth

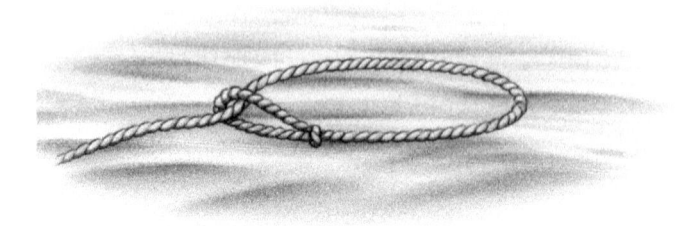

My name is Yes Gartooth of the famous Gartooths. If that gets your snout all in an uproar, so be it. I'm not about to start apologizing for who I am.

What I would like to say is that I've had it with the Three-Berry Academy for the Totally Knuckleheaded. I've been trying to pass sixth grade for twenty-two years or some such number. I've never met a river troll yet who could count past one without lying. There's nothing we do worse than count—unless it's add and subtract. Anything to do with numbers makes my tail twitch and the back of my throat go dry as roasted bark.

So far as I'm concerned, multiplication and division are pure make-believe.

We straight?

All right then.

Anyway, whatever number of years Quiet Quickthorn has been filling my head with sand, I've had it. I'm so sick and tired of school that I'm quitting. Told my mother too. She's the president of the Three-Berry Parent Association and nearly had a guppy. Tears, bar-of-soap threats, the works.

In the end, she agreed to not say a word if I helped old Quiet Quickthorn set this year's student traps. Her big idea is that I'll never resist all that bait, but if I do, then she says maybe I'm not her little tadpole anymore. But she calls that a big *if*.

That's why I'm helping old Quickthorn load all her snares, along with all the bait for those snares, into my dugout canoe. Listen, young river trolls aren't going to show up in a classroom just because some school teacher says pretty please. It takes considerably more than that to trick one of us back inside a school after a full summer of roaming free on the river.

To fill her seats, Quiet Quickthorn spends the week before the start of classes baiting snares to catch us. When she asked if I was ready to put those traps out, I jumped to my feet and grumbled, "No."

"Are my bags on board?" Quiet asked.

"No," I told her.

"Marshmallows?"

"No."

"Both bags of them?"

"No."

"One bag of big marshmallows? One small?"

"No and no."

"Perfect," Quiet said. "Then I'd say it's dark enough to be off. Agreed?"

"No."

But I climbed into my boat anyway. If you think I was going to run a rake through my hair for this little outing, forget it. I don't care what Ma wanted. I'm a Gartooth, ain't I? My teeth are as crooked as the next Gartooth's. My tail too. I'm as good as the rest of my hatch and can say NO with the best of them.

So my willow-branch hair was all gunked up. My orange eyes were all sparky. My green scales all smeared with the fresh river muck I'd been rolling in. Maybe my freckles weren't warted out yet, but I was barely seventy-five or so. A little young for that, don't you think?

"Let's go," Quiet ordered, hiking up her purple jersey to climb aboard.

So we pushed off from the Quickthorn lodge. My boat was a beautiful thing—all full of cracked shells and sticky clam juice. The paddle was a stop sign tied to a stick. We skipped across the water as fast as a motorboat.

It was a cramped ride though. Quiet's bait bags were stuffed full of exactly the kind of things that young trolls crave. And tangled beneath our feet was the rope for all the snares we'd be setting around the bait. Each length of rope kept trying to wrap itself around our tails because that's what the spell cast upon them demanded. The way we had to keep swatting nooses away slowed us plenty.

"Dead-end Slough first," Quiet called over her shoulder.

At the mouth of that slough we passed a swamp oak that Quiet liked the look of. I tied one end of the first snare to a stout branch and made the other end into a loop that I set atop a pool of water lilies fronting the tree.

"Ready?" Quiet asked.

"No."

Reaching into her bait bag, Quiet Quickthorn pulled out a single tennis shoe that was a lovely deep blue. Carefully, oh so carefully, she set it on a water lily pad at the center of the snare.

I breathed easier when I saw that. I didn't have a clamshell's worth of interest in some tennis shoe, royal blue or otherwise. The thing was too small to fit on my paws, and to be honest, didn't even have any leeches inside it.

When Quiet asked for a bag of marshmallows, I handed the nearest one over without flinching. She sprinkled the sneaker with several small marshmallows, which for a young river troll was the most delicious smelling snack this side of a clambake. Better even than candied minnows or frog eggs.

Our next stop was outside the human village of Big Rock. We set that snare in the mud in front of a culvert.

I tensed when Quiet pulled out the bait for the trap. This time I figured for sure it'd be something I couldn't resist. When she showed me a huge pair of boxer shorts that had red hearts all over them, I laughed out loud and guessed, "Mudnoses?"

That clan was known for wearing last-year's fashions.

"Maybe."

Quiet dropped a couple of marshmallows on top of the shorts and we were on our way again.

Our next stop was the old wagon wheel bridge where I baited three snares with a lawn sprinkler, empty turtle shell, and a rusty can opener.

I'm telling you, that turtle shell gave me a chill. Two or ten years ago she'd caught me with one of those. But now I was older, wiser. I didn't lift so much as a claw toward it. Finding out that I had some willpower started me humming.

"Are you singing?" Quiet snapped.

"No."

On to the Three-Soda Boat Club, where we baited one snare with the tongue from an old leather boot.

Another trap got a glow-in-the-dark tennis ball. I barely looked at either and even helped my teacher without being asked.

You're probably not going to believe this, but I was already starting to think of her as my *former* teacher. Why, I was almost enjoying myself. And my mood brightened even more when we baited snares with a baby rattle, pillow, pencil, butter knife, candy cane, tape measure, feather, fake mustache, troll doll, and red clown nose, to name a few. Not a one of them tempted me in the slightest, not even if sweetened with marshmallows.

"I suppose you're thinking you might not get caught this year," Quiet commented.

"No, Ma'am."

"I suppose you think you're ready to quit school."

"So what if I am?"

"You know the consequences of leaving early?"

She was talking about the contract that all students and parents signed before enrolling.

"It doesn't matter to me if I have to come back

after I'm dead," I bragged. "What would I be doing then anyway?"

"Typically shortsighted," Quiet Quickthorn snorted. "But I won't try to talk you out of it. Experience has taught me it's hopeless. How long have you been at the academy now, thirty-eight years?"

"Forty-eight, Ma'am."

"As if you'd know. Well, I've a couple more snares. Let's see how you do with them."

At the railroad tracks in Blue Wing, we set a snare atop a single rail. The bait was a silver Viking, which was exactly the sort of action figure that young trolls love to set on the front of their boats as prow ornaments. She even had me position it so that a nearby streetlight made it shine as if polished.

The struggle that erupted inside me was enough to shake a snail off my tongue. Twice my right paw started to reach toward the Viking. Twice my left paw held it back.

"It is rather impressive," Quiet Quickthorn agreed, admiring the Viking. "And of course whoever claims it will get to keep it forever."

"No," I weakly gasped.

And believe it or not, and I've got to say that I could barely believe it, that was the answer I stuck with. Turning around, I dragged myself back to the dugout canoe. I was totally out of breath by the time I got there, but I got there.

"It wouldn't surprise me if you double back for that one as soon as you drop me off," Quiet said.

"No," I said through clenched teeth.

"Well, help me set one last snare, and I'll let you go test that answer. I always like to put one trap near the academy, in case there's some eager student who can't wait to get started."

I mouthed No, refusing to believe that for a second. Then I paddled hard, feeling stronger the farther we got from the action figure.

The last snare was tied to a cottonwood branch that arched over the Three-Berry Academy's sunken schoolhouse. The loop floated on the water. Quiet fussed with it until she had it positioned exactly where she wanted it.

"There. That should do nicely."

"Aren't you going to bait it?" I asked.

"You know, that's always been the trouble with you, Yes Gartooth. You don't pay attention. I've already baited it."

Leaning over for a closer look, I corrected her, "Looks empty to me."

"I can't help that," Quiet said, without dropping so much as a single marshmallow in the center of the noose. "This snare is set. You're free to go."

She started to put one leg over the side of my dugout canoe.

"Are you sure?" I asked, squinting at the empty snare.

"Young troll, I've been teaching at this school for more years than I care to remember, and I've been bouncing clams off your snout for a goodly number of those years. And in all of that time have you ever known me to give an incorrect answer?"

"Yes," I said, feeling courageous. "Just now. There's no bait in that trap."

There followed a tippy pause that ended with Quiet Quickthorn asking, "Would you bet your tail on that?"

"Yes," I said. And to prove that I meant it, I reached over the side of the boat to splash the water at the center of the snare's loop. "See? Nothing. The snare's completely—"

Wouldn't you know, I never got to finish that thought. The snare floating atop the water began to close the instant I touched its center. What's more, I was so far off balance from leaning out of the boat that I couldn't pull myself back. My only chance seemed to be diving overboard and escaping through the center of the empty loop, so I took it.

I'm guessing that I wasn't the first Three-Berry student to hope I was faster than one of Quiet Quickthorn's snares. And I *almost* got away too, but almost doesn't count with anything but horseshoes and starlight, not along this stretch of river.

The snare grabbed the last thing to pass through the loop—my tail.

The instant the snare was sprung, it jerked me out of the water, flung me into the air, and dangled me over the sunken schoolhouse for all the river to see. Down below, still in the dugout canoe, Quiet Quickthorn did something quite unexpected. She tried to perk me up.

"What would you say if I told you this was for your own good?" she asked.

"Phooey!"

"Would it make you feel any better if I gave you a list of all the students who've found themselves hanging right where you are?"

"Hardly."

"Some of them are quite famous," she coaxed.

"Don't bother."

"All right then, you force my hand. What if I was to tell you that I need you in school because you're the only one who gets my jokes?"

I was about to bark NO WAY but stopped myself. I'd never known that Quiet Quickthorn made jokes. I'd always assumed that when her lower lip flipped over and quivered, and there was a crackly sound trapped in her throat, that she was snarling because someone had missed an answer.

But what if she'd been trying to grin and laugh?

What then?

Suddenly the whole school year in front of me looked better than it ever had before, and I found myself saying in disbelief, "Really?"

"Really," Quiet Quickthorn confirmed. Tilting her head so that her wandering eye could see me, she helpfully added, "And perhaps there's one other reason that I want you back."

"Yes?"

"Given your current predicament, it looks to me as though you haven't quite learned everything I have to teach you."

Tenpenny Hammertoe

Don't ask me who, but somebody pounded a spike halfway into the grass. Maybe to hold the lawn down in case of a high wind.

Or to give dragonflies a perch.

I suppose they might have been trying to build a sundial.

Or it could have been somebody's idea of a joke, from back when spikes and nails and such were new-fangled and still seemed funny. I don't know.

What I do know is that over the years river trolls have come from far and wide just to gawk at it and maybe touch it. The way sightseers crowded around that thing? It was quite a celebrity. Trolls often used it as a landmark when giving directions.

"Go until you reach the spike in the yard, then turn left. Can't miss it."

"If you've reached the spike in the yard, turn back if you can, though it's probably already too late for that."

On rainy days I think it looks kind of noble and sad, surrounded by all that wet, glistening grass without another nail in sight.

On starry nights it looks like a telescope searching the sky for an old friend.

How long had it been there? I only wish I knew. I can tell you that it's mentioned in some of the oldest stories along the river. The old nursery rhyme about dragons and milk bottles mentions it twice. General Hotten Logrot supposedly ordered his troops to retreat to the spike in the yard and not one step farther. That was way back in the Battle of the Marsh Marigolds.

All I can say is—whoever put it there pounded it in awfully hard. The human who mows the lawn always detours around that spike as if there's a spell protecting it. Many a bull troll has bragged they could yank it out with their bare paws. Many a bull troll has failed.

That's probably how the rumors about some underground beast holding onto its other end got started.

I'm not wasting time worrying about any of that. All I know is that once I get my paws on that thing, I'm going to use it to build something magnificent, something I'll be remembered for through the ages. Trolls are going to say, *That Tenpenny Hammertoe, he didn't mess around.*

That spike's the only reason I attend the Three-Berry Academy. I just got to learn how to pull it out. But so far the only thing Quiet Quickthorn's taught me about freeing spikes is to wait until there's a noose around the one you're after. She claims that ropes help loosen things up.

To be honest, so far I haven't noticed they help that much.

All I know for sure is that every time I grab hold of that thing I find myself dangling upside down from an overhanging maple faster than you can say *Barge coming!* I'm hoping that Quiet Quickthorn has something new to teach me this year.

Blaze Wrinklesnout

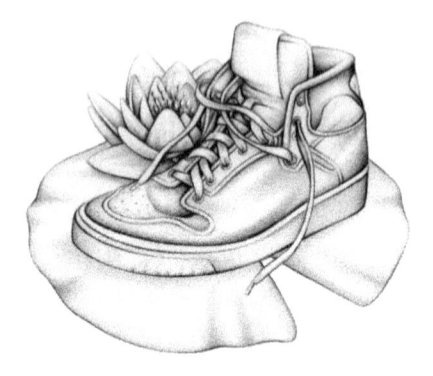

I prefer to be called Blaze Wrinklesnout, or Mr. B for short, or B if you're in a hurry, or even Heavy Load. I am a little on the extra-chunky side. But really you can call me anything, just not Ear. Everyone's always calling me Ear.

The entire week before the Three-Berry Academy opens its door I always stay inside my family's lodge where no one can see me. If my mother shoos me outside, I wiggle back in through my bedroom window as soon as no one's looking. And if it's daylight, even one of my mother's terrible muck biscuits can't drive me out the door. Of course everyone knows why I don't want to go to school. It doesn't take any genius to figure that out. We go through the same business every year.

"Where's Blaze?" Burma shouted at breakfast.

He's my oldest brother, by twenty or so minutes, and the man of the house because river troll fathers have a habit of disappearing before a hatch. If you want to find out all about that mess, some guy wrote a book called Horns & Wrinkles.

"In his room," our mother answered.

"What! On a beautiful, gloomy, sopping wet night like this? What's he doing back there?"

"Holding a pillow over his head."

"Is it that time of year already?"

"I'm afraid so, dear."

"Well you tell him . . ."

But nobody had to tell me anything. I could hear Burma's shouts just fine, even with a pillow over my head. Our lodge was on the small side.

The only one who ever has any luck talking to me when I'm holed up like this is my sister Bell, and she prefers not to bother with me unless Burma is making such a total fuss that no one can sniff straight. And right now, given the way Burma's splashing around the porridge room and threatening to let all my pet leeches go if I don't pull myself together, she's pounding on my door just to keep the peace.

"It's really not that bad," Bell promised me.

"Go away!" I shouted, holding the pillow over my head tighter than ever.

"No, really," Bell insisted. "Nobody would even notice it if you'd quit asking all the time."

Maybe there's some truth to that. My ears may be unmatched, one being half the size of the other, but it's hard to notice unless you're looking down at me from above. Large as river troll heads are, it's almost impossible to see both of our ears at once.

But hey, when you live underwater there's a lot of trolls swimming above you all the time, and you can't tell me that some of them aren't looking down every once and a while. I've been sensitive as a shell-less turtle about my ears ever since a classmate got mad at me for sharing one of my mother's terrible muck biscuits and called me the first nasty thing that popped into her head—*Small Ear*. Everyone had soon shortened that to Ear.

"I don't believe you."

"No need to go all huffy," Bell said.

"Oh yah?" I shouted. "How would you like to be called Ear everywhere you went?"

"Now that's not true. There's plenty who don't call you that."

"Name one."

"Me."

"You don't count. Name somebody at the Three-Berry, besides the teacher."

"I don't go to your school. How would I know?"

"Exactly."

"Now Blaze, everybody's a little different."

"Not when it comes to ears."

"What do you care what they think, anyway?"

"I don't!" I yelled.

From the hallway, Bell suggested, "Maybe if you covered it up . . ."

"I tried that."

"With a rusty tin can? That only drew more attention to it. Try something pretty."

"Like what?"

"How should I know? It's not my ear."

"That's what I keep trying to tell you."

And so on, until Burma got tired of listening to us, barged into my room, and grabbed my leech boot. That spongy, mossy old thing was my pride and glory, all full of pet leeches with names like Tooth, Chomper, and Fang.

"Enough!" Burma shouted. "You can't stay in here forever. I'm sick and tired of watching you mope around. School starts tomorrow. And ear or no ear, you're going."

Shaking his tail at me, he pushed off for our

lodge's front door, which of course was underwater, and flung my boot outside.

"Why you—"

But I didn't have time to finish my threat. I was too busy diving after my boot.

The instant I left the lodge, my brother slammed the door shut behind me and bolted it. He then raced down our lodge's main hall to shutter up all the bedroom windows too.

So even though I sniffed out my boot before many of the leeches escaped, and by the way, I've collected some real beauties, including a rare corkscrew one that I had to send away for, I found myself locked out of my own home. No amount of whacking my tail against the door or throwing clams at the shutters did me any good either.

I had to satisfy myself with shouting insults, which is the general way us river trolls carry on. But I was so upset that I couldn't think of anything original to call them, which made me madder than a dry mudpuppy.

"Rock trolls!" I bellowed. "Guppy brains! Peppermint breaths!"

And a lot more of the same piffle until I was hoarse. Pretty standard stuff.

Of course everyone inside the lodge was busy tossing back insults of their own. That lasted until I'd heard enough and decided to swim away, never to return. I told myself I'd be better off throwing together a nice little hut on some backwater where no one would ever bother me about the size of my ears again. I'd stay up all night whenever I wanted to and learn to cook muck biscuits the right way.

And anything else I felt like doing? Well, I'd do that too.

Passing by an island, I came up out of the river to roll around in the sand a bit. That always settled me down and helped me think.

My brother was right about one thing—it was a lovely, gloomy night. Not that'd I'd ever admit it out loud, not to someone who didn't have to go to school. As the oldest of the hatch, Burma had gone directly into the family business of net-cutting without having to worry about the size of his ears, which weren't exactly identical either. And my sister Bell, she was lucky enough to go to a school where everyone had too much fun peeling bark for baskets to bother looking at less-than-perfect ears.

But just when I was about to tackle all the other reasons I have for feeling mistreated, put-upon, and generally worthless, a bright light flashed across my eyes, freezing me.

For an instant I panicked, thinking I'd stayed up past daybreak, but the light quickly moved on and soothing darkness returned. The blinding glare had come from a barge, sweeping its spotlight about in search of channel markers.

Something a dozen feet away from me stood out as the beam passed over it. Resting atop a bed of lily pads was a single tennis shoe. It was a lovely royal blue and looked as if lost by a big-footed basketball star. The way my sister Bell loved to gush on about such footwear, you might think she was talking about catfish whiskers or a bucket of priceless mud.

How something so valuable had landed on a lily pad in the middle of the Mississippi wasn't anything I bothered to think twice about. Floodwaters, no doubt. Besides, I was too busy remembering something that Bell had mentioned to worry about where the slipper had come from.

Cover it up with something pretty.

At that moment I saw how to keep everyone from noticing anything about my ears. Covering my shrimpy ear with a beautiful blue sneaker ought to do the trick.

It wasn't until I reached for the shoe that it dawned on me in a whip-lashing hurry that I'd once again be attending the Three-Berry Academy for the Totally Gifted. That's when the snare's noose closed around my tail, yanking me upward.

From my new height, I could see a gang of preschool trolls tromping my way, and I quickly hid my small ear beneath the tennis shoe. When the youngsters reached me, they all stopped, bumping into each other as they gawked upwards.

"I wish I had a reason to wear something like that," one of them said, pointing at the blue sneaker.

"Me too," added another.

"Do you think a rock troll bit off his ear?" asked a third. "Is that why he's wearing that thing?"

"Could be. Or a wizard might have bought it from him. I hear they'll pay serious clams for a good troll ear."

"Maybe a lighting bolt sizzled the side of his head."

"Or a monster leech got him."

"Hey mister," the leader of the young trolls asked, "what do you have under that shoe, anyway?"

"None of your business," I answered.

"You're not that guy they call Ear, are you?"

"So what if I am?"

"Nothing. Only we were wondering if you could tell us where to get an ear covering as cool as yours."

"No way," I told them. "I'm the only one who gets to wear one of these."

And for once the wait to be collected for school didn't seem so endless.

Two Shellcruncher

Don't be shocked, but I am the one and only Two Shellcruncher. I've yellow eyes, was named after a number, and am by far the brightest student to ever attend that little one-turtle school that some call the Three-Berry Academy for the Totally Gifted. Just ask me.

"Even smarter than Arithmetic Icksome?"

"Way."

"Booky Undermuck too?"

"Poor Booky. His attempts to outdo me are nothing but sad and doomed."

"What about Smuch Lipsmacker?"

"Oh please!"

Even my mother has to admit I'm one smart cookie, though she only says it when I'm out of the room. In public she refuses to say anything of the kind. What troll mother would? Although when I passed first grade in a handful of years, easily setting a school record, she did make a point of letting my aunts and uncles know. Never again though.

The way I steamed through the next bunch of grades, reaching the top one in slightly less than somewhere around twenty-seven or ninety-seven years? She claims I'm impossible to live with.

Well, that's what she gets for having such a brilliant child. No matter what my mother does, I have suggestions on how she can do it better and in half the time.

And if my mother tries to convince me otherwise? Well, I certainly don't waste any time shredding whatever advice is headed my way.

There are plenty of troll mothers who'd gag a daughter like me with riverweed just to get some peace and quiet. Quite a few of them have also publicly said that my mother's only gotten what she deserved. Naming a hatchling after a number is asking for trouble.

She's never dared stuff anything in my mouth though. I think she's secretly proud of my accomplishments.

Oh, sometimes she may wish her little light bulb

didn't have to burn so brightly, and I've even heard her tell her friends over a morning cup of slough tea, "Thank goodness for school. If she was around here all day long, I swear I'd chop off my tail."

But she's always the first one to mention what grade I'm in and how quickly I got there.

That's why she had to sit down when I announced I was all done with school.

"W-what?"

"I am in the top grade now, Mother. Except for Booky Undermuck no one else is even close to that, and he's been going to that school for close to a thousand years. Maybe more."

That wasn't exactly true. Booky had only been attending Three-Berry for somewhere around seventy or thirty years, and last spring Artum Smokesclam and Pearly Leechlicker had clawed their way into the grade just before the top, though that was no guarantee that they'd stay there.

Students had been known to backslide over summer vacation.

"Mother," I scolded, "the Three-Berry Academy is only a school for the *totally* gifted. I should be attending one for the *extremely* gifted, if there was such a place, which there isn't. That's why I see no reason for me to waste any more time in school. There's just nothing more for me to learn there. My nights would be better spent here at home, studying on my own."

"Then why," my mother squeaked, doing her best not to panic, "did your teacher send a reminder that she was expecting you back this fall?"

"That old fuddy-duddy. She just doesn't like empty seats."

"I'll have you know she's a highly thought of teacher. Why do you think we send you there?"

"Oh I suppose you mean well enough," I said with an airy wave of my paw, giving her the benefit of the doubt, "but really, Mother, half the class hasn't made it out of first grade. What's that tell you?"

That wasn't an argument she wanted to hear me replay again. Instead, she tried her luck elsewhere. "That birthday counter over in Big Rock puts you at fifty-seven. Much too young to be done with school."

"Who says?"

"Anyone you care to ask."

"As I live and breathe." I sucked down a deep, heavy breath, and took a long gaze up toward the top of the river, where a sprinkle of starlight twinkled through the ripples and eddies above us. "I hate to break this to you, Mother, but some of us have better things to do with our nights than listen to first graders learn the difference between tadpoles and minnows."

"Are you trying to tell me that you don't feel the tiniest pull from the bait your teacher puts out for you?"

"That old stuff? Not a single tug."

"Prove it."

Up until now that trick had never failed. Proving something required brainpower, and I never could resist showing off how smart I was.

But this year I'd vowed to myself that things would be different.

Later that night, after my other hatchmates had been drawn topside by the delicious scent of frog eggs and catfish spawn and clam juice and marshmallows and whatever other goodies were used to entice students at other schools, my mother and I toured baited snares along the riverbank. There wasn't any need to call them anything but traps, not with a top grader like me, and I spurned each and every one we happened upon.

Many of the snares hadn't even been set by the Three-Berry Academy, but my mother was getting desperate to find some way—any way—to get me back to school.

"How about that one?" she asked, pointing at something pink beneath a marsh pepper. It was short and flat with a marshmallow atop it.

"An eraser?" I said. "It'll take more than that, Mother."

"If you're so smart, tell me what it's used for."

"Plugging ears."

"What else?"

"Sometimes noses."

I really was a little know-it-all. Mother moved on.

"Over there?" she pointed. "What's that?"

"A ball, Mother. Really, I'm surprised that Quiet Quickthorn ever let you out of that school."

"I can see it's a ball," she came right back. "But what are all those different colors painted on it?"

"Who knows? Human stuff. There's no telling why they do things. I've heard they don't even call it a ball. They say it's a globe. And get this, they seem to think they live on it somewhere. With ideas like that clogging up their ears, how they ever make it through breakfast is a mystery to me."

"Where did you hear all that, may I ask?"

"The other night. Down by the crumbly old bridge."

"I thought you'd been told to stay away from there?"

We disagreed about that until our snouts drew us to another baited snare that was just rotten with marshmallows.

"I suppose you've seen one of these before too," my mother said, acting as if she'd listened more than long enough to me prattling on about all the things I knew. She sounded as if ready to ship me off to some school for rock trolls.

"Certainly," I answered without slowing. "Some kind of box."

I may have made a little mistake there. My mother might have noticed that I sounded a little steamed about this one and was maybe doing my best to shove on past it. That only made her all the curiouser.

"I wonder what those buttons are for?" she speculated.

The box had a row of square buttons with letters printed above them that were arranged this way:

STOP REWIND FORWARD PLAY

Don't ask me what they said. I may be a genius but even geniuses have limits. The letters did make it clear that this was something human-made though. Just to be on the safe side, Mother backed off a step with me.

"Honestly, Mother. You act as if you've never seen a button before."

"Why don't you try pushing one of them?"

"Not me."

"Are you afraid of it?"

"Nice try, Mother. But I can see the snare around it too, you know."

"Oh, well, if that's what's bothering you, allow me."

She hunted up a long stick and used it to push a

button while standing well outside the snare's reach. The button she chose had the letters **REWIND** printed above it, and the instant she touched it, the box began hissing like a snake. We both jumped back.

"Try that button there," I squealed, pointing at one with **STOP** printed above it. I maybe knew a little more about that box than I cared to admit.

The hissing stopped when she poked the button I was pointing at.

"Well," Mother huffed. "That's humans for you. Why would they put a snake inside a box?"

"They may have had a reason," I darkly cautioned.

"I'd like to know what."

"Maybe to scare off frogs," I reasoned, edging even farther away from the thing. "Come on, Mother. I smell something better up ahead."

"What do you think would happen if I try that button?" my mother asked, pointing out one with **PLAY** printed above it.

"Probably nothing," I blurted, maybe a little too fast to be convincing.

As soon as Mother pressed the button a voice began to speak, and not any snake or even a human voice either. My mother tensed until recognizing that it was my teacher, Quiet Quickthorn, who was speaking, though her usual strong voice sounded fuzzy and far away. That may have been because it was coming out of the box.

If the Three-Berry's headmistress was trapped in there, she was beyond rescue, although my old teacher hardly sounded bothered by being shrunken down to that size. In fact, she was patiently repeating something, the way she did when teaching a difficult lesson.

"After one comes . . . ?"

At which point her voice trailed off as if trying to coax an answer out of a student. There was a pause that lasted about as long as it takes a sunning turtle to blink, and then the headmistress repeated herself more firmly.

"After one comes . . .?"

And then another voice answered.

"Five?"

My mother gasped and buried her snout under her arm. All right, I'll admit it—the voice that answered might have sounded an awful lot like mine. But of course it couldn't be me inside that box because I was standing right next Mother, waving frantically for her to punch another button. That wasn't going to happen, not with Mother thinking she was onto something.

"No-o," the Quiet Quickthorn in the box said. "Try again. After one comes . . .?"

"Eight?" I answered from inside the box.

"Now you're guessing," Quiet cautioned. "And guessing doesn't count, not even if you're right. Which you're not. Now think! After one comes . . .?"

This time there was such a long pause that my mother lifted her head and whispered as if the Quiet Quickthorn in the box might overhear. "Is she teaching you to count?"

I took a deep breath before spilling the minnows. "Was."

"Was?"

"Last spring. That's when we said all that stuff."

"Oh my," Mother said, clearly shocked at such doings.

Not that hearing something spoken several months ago was a total surprise, not along a stretch of river so thick with spells and charms as ours. But the idea that Quiet Quickthorn was trying to teach me to count—that stole her breath away.

Trolls can't count any better than they can read. Worse, actually.

We know the names of all kinds of numbers, especially between one and one hundred, but we don't have much of an idea on how to string them together. The idea that numbers could be added together usually brought shouts of *liar* from the back of a classroom. I've been known to join in too. And just mentioning the word *subtraction* sent half of most classes diving beneath their desks. Multiplication? Division? Geometry? Only a brave fool brought them up around a river troll.

So now I had a mother—my mother!—gawking at me with a little awe and perhaps a touch of fear.

No river troll in history had ever come close to figuring out how to count. Just the fact that Quiet Quickthorn thought I might have a chance at it—well, my mother had no idea I was so brilliant. For the first time I think it actually occurred to her that maybe I really shouldn't be wasting my time in school.

"Fifteen?" I guessed from inside the box.

My mother couldn't have looked prouder than if a snapping turtle had laid a clutch of eggs atop our lodge.

My reaction was different. I was busy remembering the day Quiet Quickthorn had decided to find out if I was anywhere near as smart as I liked to think. My teacher had quizzed me all morning. It went on for so long that the other students started hooting at every answer I offered up, making me feel so stubborn that I'd even challenged my teacher, saying she probably didn't know the right answer herself.

Quiet Quickthorn had briskly informed me that every certified teacher in the valley knew the answer to what came after one. It was presented to them with their teaching certificate, in case someday a student really did know the answer.

And if a teacher thought a student might have a

shot at actually counting, they were told to come get the box that now stood before me and my mother, so that proof of their achievement could be recorded.

"So what comes after one?" Quiet repeated from inside the box.

"Thirty-six," I guessed from inside the box.

Then came another voice from inside the box, a loud, obnoxious voice that belonged to that Mudd Sloughless who always sat at the back of the class and could only tell the difference between a minnow and a tadpole by licking them. "You already—"

But I couldn't bear to hear that lout say that I'd already guessed that number, not in front of my mother. I couldn't stand being humiliated that way and blindly jabbed at the buttons on the box, aiming for the letters that said **STOP**.

Too late did I recall what else would happen. My tail was caught by the snare in nothing flat and up into the tree above us I flew.

Down below, my mother breathed a huge sigh of relief, for it appeared that her daughter was once again headed back to the Three-Berry Academy for the Totally Gifted.

Who knows, maybe this is the year I will learn how to count.

Nod Logrot

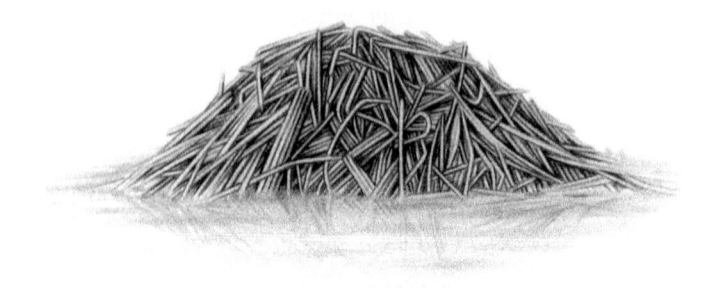

Us Logrots come from a long line of sleepers, all right? So there's not a one of us who doesn't take great pride in our lodges. Who wants a roof caving in on you in the middle of a good nap?

Seen from above, a river troll's lodge looks like a huge muskrat house, all reeds and branches that are piled higgledy-piggledy in a heap.

Beneath that messy roof it doesn't get any neater. Housekeeping is better left for when you're dead is how river trolls usually put it. And us Logrots like to add that when you're alive you could be sleeping.

The above-water parts of our lodge include a large kitchen for that rare meal that requires cooking. Every troll knows that fires work best when they're not wet.

We've got a summer dining room, sometimes called a porridge room, right next the kitchen. That way whoever's stuck cooking has a chance at the eats before they're all gobbled up.

Table manners are generally frowned upon, especially if we have guests. The best way to make a visitor feel at home is to elbow him or her aside and sweep the nearest platter of food into your mouth. Chewing comes later.

Picking your teeth with a fish bone comes even later, after a nap.

But it's the part of a lodge that's underwater where you can tell the most about a troll clan. Take our living room, it's always totally submerged. Who wants to use your lungs when you have gills?

As for furniture, how's a half-dozen lumpy couches sound? We also keep a goodly number of soft-shell turtles, what some call leatherbacks, on hand for pillows and footstools. Comfort's the thing.

We don't worry about there being no lights either. For one thing they keep you awake, and anyway, our orange eyes like it best when it's deep-water dark.

If you need a little dimness, there's always foxfire. Smearing the walls with that stuff lends a ghostly green to everything, a sight that can be quite lovely, if you go in for that sort of thing. Whenever our lodge has been recently smeared, its windows and doors shine like underwater beacons. But even lodges that haven't been touched up for years can still light up a backwater like moon glow.

Our underwater windows and doors are rarely closed, so river water circulates freely, keeping our lodge fresh, which is the best way to sleep. Better yet, schools of crappies, bluegills, or sunnies pass through and help clean up the table crumbs while we're snoozing.

Home entertainment includes cracking open clams, sniffing a good book, or watching dinner swim by.

Of course we keep some fish as pets. Dog- and catfish are favorites, 'cause they like to sleep almost as much as we do. No buffalo fish though. The way they bang around can make it almost impossible to keep your eyes closed.

Finally, our lodge has plenty of bedrooms. You can never have enough of them.

When the mood for a snooze hits, you don't want to have to waste time hunting for a bedroom. You want one NOW!

Stars and sand, there's nothing that refreshes a

troll's soul like thirty to forty hours of good shuteye with your favorite painted turtle curled up on your chest.

And please keep in mind that as poorly as us river trolls count, thirty or forty hours might last a week or two, especially if you're talking about us Logrots.

We take our sleep that seriously.

There's not a one of us who isn't always yawning and sleepy-eyed, with river gunk gumming up our nostrils. Most nights we're too busy snoring to wake up and blow our noses.

Nope, we're champion snoozers, one and all. Got the carp-scale pillows to prove it too.

But the one who leaves all of us yawning at the gate is my uncle, Rip Van Logrot. He once slept through a pirate bombardment that sent a cannonball crashing into our roof.

And even Rip Van's reputation as the best sleeper in the clan isn't secure, not so long as I'm around.

They call me Nod, and I've been gaining on him since the day I was hatched. My clan's expecting big things from me.

I slept through the afternoon I was hatched. Unheard of.

Hatchlings normally spend the first several weeks squick-squawking in the nest, wanting to be fed.

Not me.

Some days I don't even wake up to eat. Deeply unheard of.

Trolls have come from miles away just to watch me sleep through the Mid-Summer Ooze, and river celebrations don't get much louder than that, what with exploding puffballs and swimming bands and who-who shouting contests all over the backwaters.

So it shouldn't come as any surprise that I've made it my goal to stay home and sleep through my first month of school at the Three Berry Academy. When Rip Van Logrot heard about that, he sleepwalked into my bedroom to shake me by the tail and bugle into my ear with a large-mouth bass who doubles as a trumpet.

I smiled, rolled over, slumbered on.

Hey, I was dreaming about a young river troll who looked exactly like me and who was dreaming, which for me was the happiest kind of dream. The ones that happen when you're asleep, I mean.

Daydreams have never done much for me. The troll in my dream had found a comfy mud hole to curl up in, and that had him smiling too. And I knew why. The troll in my dream, who looked exactly like me, was also dreaming.

He was dreaming of another troll who looked exactly like me, who was dreaming of another troll who looked exactly like me, and so on, until at the very end of that line of trolls who looked exactly like me and were dreaming of another troll who looked exactly like me—at the end of all that was one last troll who was dreaming of our favorite snack—turtle shell stuffed full of marshmallows.

He dreamed it was waiting for him just outside his mud hole. The aroma of marshmallows had his snout happily bubbling away.

Finally the last dreamer in line sniffed himself awake. I watched him stretch and yawn as if he'd been asleep for a year and a half on a bed of cattail reeds.

After all that time he woke up starving and fell on a bowl of marshmallows beside his bed as if they were the last bites of food in the world. Which in my dream within a dream, within a dream, they were.

But the instant that last troll who looked exactly like me touched those marshmallows, he discovered they were the bait in a snare, one that closed around his tail and whipped him upwards to hang upside-down from a dream tree that had golden leaves.

Every other dreaming troll who looked exactly me got whipped upwards too, one after another, right out of the dream they were part of, to dangle from that dream tree. A slight breeze made them all jingle like a pouch full of treasure.

My nose told me that every leaf on that dream tree had been rubbed with a wonderful clam-and-snail juice polish. And what's more, the birds in that tree were . . .

I didn't get to find out the rest of that remarkable tree's secrets because about then I discovered that what was happening to all the Nods in the dream was also happening to me, in the waking world. A snare had tightened around my tail too. It was pulling me right out my bedroom window and hoisting me into a crabapple tree whose fruit was a beautiful golden red.

How Quiet Quickthorn ever managed to bait a snare in my dream was a question that never got answered. She wasn't the sort to share trade secrets.

Whether Rip Van Logrot had a hand in placing the snare in my dream would have been another question worth asking, if any of my relatives could have stayed awake long enough to do it.

As for me, I'm awake.

It's impossible for even a Logrot as talented as me to sleep while hanging upside down by my tail. Looks like my plans for sleeping through the first month of school were nothing but a dream.

Mudd Dimwater

"So I saw this huge ball of twine and grabbed it. And here I am."

"Wait a minute. There's got to be something more to it than that. Didn't you notice the twine was bait in a snare?"

"Natch. Do I look dense?"

"Hard to tell, with both of us hanging upside-down by our tails the way we are, ten feet off the ground. But maybe you could answer me this—if you knew what it was, why'd you grab it?"

"Needed it."

"All of it? That's a lot of twine."

"Needed every last inch of it. How else do you think my clan would find their way to my school?"

"Now why would they want to find your school? My mother says that the last thing she wants to know is where my school is."

"Because they have to come tip over any fishing boats that go drifting over the school."

"What for?"

"Have you ever been sitting in class trying to memorize something important, like say all the kinds of minnows, or which grubs are poisonous, and you hear a ker-plop, followed by a big juicy night crawler that comes swinging by your classroom windows on a hook?"

"Of course I have. What's that got to do with anything?"

"Did the teacher like it?"

"Not in this lifetime."

"Well, that's why my school pays my clan to chase fishermen off."

"Bet your classmates just love you."

"Tons. But working for free's the only way my clan can afford to send me there."

"You mean they have to pay for these schools they send us to?"

"Do fish jump? Though maybe they don't pay for

the school so much as the teacher. If you don't cough up for the teacher, you don't get picked for the school, so it all amounts to the same thing."

"I'll bet that's why they couldn't buy me a new boat this year. My old one's heavy and slow as the month of July."

"At least you got one."

"I guess. So you come from a bunch of boat tippers?"

"And anything else that needs tipping. We do some fish-line snipping too, with anchor collecting on the side. And we've got the Fish Society contract for this stretch of river."

"The what?"

"Fish Society. You probably know it by its full name, the Keep All Mississippi River Fish for Mississippi River Trolls Society. Around here we shorten it to Fish Society so that we don't have to remember all the extra words."

"Oh, sure. I've heard of them."

"I should hope so. Without it the humans would be catching all the river's fish, and then what would we have on our dinner plates?"

"Sounds right. Hey, I always thought that tipping boats sounded like the life for me. I come from a bunch of lodge and hut builders, so we're always tail deep in mud and sticks and sand. But say, why do you even have to go to school? I thought boat tippers just went out and did stuff."

"The feud."

"What feud?"

"You must be new to this stretch of river."

"So what if I am?"

"Nothing. Nothing. No need to be so touchy. It's just that everyone around here knows about the feud. I'm a Dimwater, see, and that means I can't smell a thing."

"It does?"

"Thanks to the feud. Ever heard of Roll'em Jones?"

"Isn't he some kind of wizard?"

"Yup. And he stole my clan's sense of smell. Keeps it in a mayonnaise jar right next to a glass of eyeballs that watch everything and a box of shrunken heads that never shut up. Makes it impossible to steal back."

"But why'd he take it in the first place?"

"Gambling debts, which we refused to pay because he runs a crooked game at that parlor of his."

"I've heard that. But what's all this have to do with your going to school?"

"Only everything. The first thing we did, after he swiped our sniffers, I mean, is take an ad out in the Blue Wing Bugler that called him a four-flushing cheater."

"How'd he take that?"

"Sent a plague of fishflies our way."

"What'd you do then?"

"Hired some hotshot elf to turn him into a dungless dung beetle."

"Hoo boy. Then what happened?"

"He sent one of his toads to the Fish Society to accuse us of padding our boat-flip count."

"Were you?"

"Not much. But now they make us take pictures of everything we flip over or they won't pay."

"Geez. That sounds rough."

"You're telling me. We can barely put duck potatoes and river cabbage in our bowls. And much as that elf charged us, you'd think his spell would have lasted for two or three lifetimes."

"It didn't?"

"Nope. Barely a day, though we've heard that Roll'em still smells a little barnyardy. That's something, I guess, but now he's picking us off one-by-one. Just last year he turned my great aunt Tar-and-grub into a glass of water that got served to the mayor of Blue Wing."

"That was your aunt?"

"Yup. So a ways back us Dimwaters held a lodge meeting and decided we had to do something drastic, like send someone to school to see if they could figure some way out of this mess. We drew grubs to see who."

"And you lost?"

"Now you're catching on. When we found out we'd have to pay the teacher, I thought maybe I was saved, but then they worked out a deal with the teacher to keep her classroom clear of fishermen and I was doomed. There still was one problem though—without our sense of smell nobody could find their way to the school if any fishermen did show up, so I thought maybe I was saved again. But the teacher I've got, she came up with this ball of twine I'm holding. I just start unraveling it when they come to pick me up for school. One end of it's tied to our lodge, the other end I knot to my desk, and whenever there's any boat tipping that needs doing, all I have to do is give the twine a tug and they follow it to school."

"So you knew what the twine was for but picked it up anyway?"

"Shhhh! Keep that to yourself, would you?"

"But why would you do something like that? We're talking about school."

"Sometimes they serve leech stew for lunch."

"Big whoop. There must be something else."

"Can you keep a secret?"

"Every time."

"This school they're sending me to? The Three-Berry Academy? It's not so bad. I mean, it's tough, but fair. And you really do learn some neat stuff."

"Like what?"

"Seeing five turtles at sunrise means the river's on the rise. Handy things like that."

"Sounds made up to me. Has this academy taught you to count that high? Say yes to that and I might start believing this Three-Berry's something special."

"Maybe not yet. But I've only been going there six or twenty years. Or maybe eight. Who knows when it comes to numbers? I'm thinking that when I hit the next grade I'll start learning the good stuff."

"I wouldn't count on it."

"Why not?"

"Schools are always saying stuff like that. To get you come back next year."

"How do you know?"

"Let's just call it an educated guess."

Boom Halfsnout

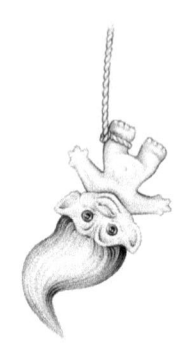

"So if you're so educated, what kind of bait did they put out for you?"

"Who said they put out bait?"

"You're hanging upside down with me, aren't you?"

"I guess so."

"So what kind of bait?"

"I forget."

"Isn't it right there in your paw?"

"Nope."

"So why'd you just whip your paw behind your back?"

"Didn't."

"Sure looked like you did."

"Maybe you better have your eyes tested."

"Oh I will. You too on the first night of school. Quiet Quickthorn doesn't leave any room for excuses. When she holds something up, you better be able to see it. Say, why are you switching schools?"

"Who says I am?"

"I do. You sure weren't at the Three-Berry last year, and you don't sound like any first grader."

"Oh. Well, I'd rather not say."

"Something bad, huh?"

"Depends what you think is bad."

"What school were you going to?"

"Doesn't matter."

"Why not?"

"It's not around anymore."

"What happened to it?"

"Big explosion."

"How'd that happen?"

"Grub class."

"What happened there?"

"If I told you I didn't know, would you drop it?"

"I guess . . . And now you're going to our school. Your whole clan's moving here?"

"Nope. They sent me up here to look after an aunt."

"All by yourself?"

"You see anyone else hanging upside-down with us?"

"What kind of help's your aunt need?"

"The none-of-your-business kind. Does everyone at this Three-Berry place ask so many questions?"

"Some more. Wait till you meet Booky. He'll drown you with 'em."

"You can't drown a river troll."

"Don't count on it. Not when it comes to Booky. So are you going to tell me what you're hiding behind your back or not?"

"Depends."

"On?"

"Whether you can keep a secret."

"Every day of the week."

"But for how long?"

"I've been known to keep one for most of an afternoon."

"Won't do."

"You're afraid to let me see, aren't you?"

"If I tell you what it is, will you quit pestering me?"

"Maybe."

"Not good enough."

"OK. I won't say another word, if you'll tell me

your name too."

"Who said anything about that?"

"I did. Just now. It's only fair. You know mine."

"No I don't. Just that you're a Dimwater. There's probably hundreds of them plugging up holes between here and the Boot and Shoe."

"Boot and Shoe? Is that where you're from?"

"I never said—"

"Mudd."

'Huh?"

"That's my first name. Mudd Dimwater. Now what's yours?"

"You're a pip."

"Thanks. I guess. So what's your name?"

"Glorious Tattletale."

"Really?"

"What do you think?"

"That you're lying, but I guess it'll do for now. So Glorious Tattletale, what's behind your back?"

"Why's it matter?"

"I just like to know what kind of troll I'm hanging upside-down with, that's all."

"Well, if you must know, it's a stick of dynamite."

"Very funny."

"Who's joking?"

"Quiet Quickthorn would never use something that dangerous for bait."

"How do you know?"

"She won't even let us sharpen our claws at school, and all of a sudden she's going to put out a brick of dynamite? I don't think so."

"Who said anything about a brick? I said stick. I'll bet you don't even know what a stick of dynamite is, do you?"

"Do too. It's one of those ka-blewy things that humans have and rock trolls are always trying to get."

"Oh so now you're an expert on rock trolls too? Next you'll be telling me you've stomped on Bodacious Deepthink's big toe."

"You think I'm crazy? I wouldn't go anywhere near that rock troll's big toe."

"Hey! Quit swinging back and forth like that. You'll knock us both out of this tree."

"I'm just trying to see what's behind your back."

"Well you better stop or this school might get blown up too."

"With that? That's nothing but one of those goofy troll dolls that humans give their kids. Yuk. They don't look anything at all like us, and they sure don't look anything like a brick of dynamite. You're nothing but a big, water-gulping liar. I'll bet that's why you had to leave that other school."

"So what if it is? At least I don't have to unravel a ball of twine all the way to school."

"No, the only thing anyone has to unravel around you is the truth."

"Say . . . you know what? I like the sound of that."

"You do?"

"You've got a way with words, don't you? How about if we have a truce?"

"I guess. I mean, since we're hanging here side-by-side and all, why not. And I'll tell you what, I won't mention any of this stuff if you don't bring up my ball of twine. Some of those older trolls at the Three-Berry sort of like to thump me about it."

"Deal."

"How do I know I can trust you?"

"What if I tell you my real name? Would that do?"

"I guess."

"Fair enough. Boom Halfsnout at your service."

"No way."

"Didn't I just say it was?"

"I'm not buying it."

"Suit yourself. I'm not begging."

"That'd make you the kid who blew up that wing dam school down by Toebright Slough."

"So?"

"He's a living legend. They say he blew that school so high that rock and clamshells and chalkboard rained down for days and gave everybody a white rash."

"Not true."

"Oh yah? So what's that white spot on your forehead?"

"Birthmark."

"First white one I've ever seen. And I heard that kid blew everything up with nothing but a bleach bottle filled full of gunk that he mixed up and topped off with some kind of spell he stole from a gnome."

"That gnome gave it to me fair and square."

"Save it! What gnome ever gave anything away fair and square?"

"This one did. I had to guard his rutabagas for a month."

"Got an answer for everything, don't you? Well answer me this. Did you get caught trying to pass some note so full of a mush it made everyone sick for a week?"

"Where'd you hear that?"

"Word gets around. Everyone says that's why Boom Halfsnout blew his school up. If you're that Boom Halfsnout, prove it."

"How?"

"What was in the note?"

"If it will make you happy. Squashed toadstools are yummy, Squished duckweed is too, a kiss from Sweetpea Carpalot, sticks stronger than glue."

"Holy . . . it is you. Did that teacher really make you read that out loud in front of the whole school?"

"He tried."

"What do you mean—tried?"

"The school blew up before he could."

"I get it. I'd have done the same thing. Wait till everybody hears who I've been hanging upside down with. I'll have friends coming out my ears."

"Hold on now. You promised I could trust you all the way to the bottom of the river and beyond."

"I never said you could trust me that far, and even if I had, that was before I knew what kind of secret you were lugging around. Something this big could eat me alive if I don't get it out."

"Tough luck. You gave your word. And if I can't count on you to keep your word, maybe I'll just blow us up right here, right now. That'd give your pals something to talk about."

"You wouldn't dare."

"Why not? If I can't be near Sweetpea, what's the use of going on?"

"Geez. You sound crazy as some moon doggy. All right, I'll keep it all to myself, even if it means I might explode."

"You better."

"I will, if you'll answer me one little question."

"What?"

"When you say her kisses are stronger than glue, just what kind of glue are we talking about?"

"Lilytongue's Till-the-end-of-time."

"You mean the stuff in the red tube?"

"I do."

"Ouch. Those kisses must really be something. She got any sisters?"

"Not so's you'd notice."

"That's a relief."

"Now I got a question for you."

"Shoot."

"How'd this teacher of yours know I'd reach out for this troll doll?"

"They say she asks the Crowleg sisters what will nab us."

"Are you talking about the sisters who can see weeks and years and months into the future? How's she afford them?"

"They graduated from Three-Berry, so they give her some kind of special discount."

"Do you think those sisters would tell her if they saw any explosions in her school's future?"

"Oh yah, they'd spill the beans. Those old hags get a real kick out of peeking in the school windows to watch us squirm in our seats, same as they once had to."

"That must mean I don't get around to blowing this one up. Wonder why. You got any pretty girls up here?"

"What kind of question's that? You better not be thinking of trotting out any more of that toadstools-are-yummy stuff. You do that and I just might blow the place up myself."

"No need to be so touchy."

"There are limits."

"OK. OK. I'll look for something else to help me get through this year. You got any nettle fields up here?"

"Plenty."

"Well I ought to be all right then. A good field of nettles can go a long way when times are tough."

"You can say that again."

Kazoo Ripp

I'm Kazoo Ripp, of the somewhat famous door-to-door Ripps, and my Granny Spoon always said, "A bowl doesn't fill itself, you know."

That was her way of letting me know I should help myself to the slumgullion that was always simmering in her kitchen kettle.

But I also figured that Granny Spoon meant a good deal more by it too. My granny was one of those wise and slightly scary old trolls who smelled of major horseradish, and talked back to floods, and tossed out about a hundred old sayings a day, some of which stuck when you first heard them, and others that didn't sneak up on you until years later.

Stuff like, *Never lick a mushroom.*

Or, *Whirlpools for snail stains.*

As a matter of fact, one of Granny Spoon's sayings, the one about bowls never filling themselves, had just caught up with me. I was taking a twilight dip on Sand-Flea Slough and had spotted a small white bowl on the riverbank. I set course for it right away, to check it out.

Empty.

But thanks to Granny Spoon, I knew that bowls didn't fill themselves, so I settled in to see who would fill this one.

I watched that bowl long enough for whippoorwills to start calling to each other in the woods around the slough.

The last threads of daylight snapped.

The growing darkness made the white bowl seem to shine all the more, as if it was releasing every bit of the light it'd collected during the day.

By then I'd grown tired of waiting to see who would fill the bowl. By then I'd started wondering if this might be a bowl worth selling with nothing in it.

I come from a family of door-to-door sales trolls who have sold everything from raindrop strainers to eyeglasses that let you see no-see-'ems.

My own name came from a carton of kazoos that

my father sold out in nothing flat, peddling them as turtle callers.

And now something told me that an empty bowl ought to be worth something, especially if I mentioned Granny Spoon's old bit about bowls not filling themselves.

If anyone wanted to know who would be filling the bowl, I'd go all secretive and give them a wink, that famous Ripp family wink, as I whispered that I'd taken a pledge not to reveal anything.

But in the next breath, I'd also let slip that whoever filled that bowl might be famous. If that didn't hook them, I wasn't a Ripp.

If anyone wanted to know what the bowl would be filled with, I'd wag a claw as if to say *Uh, uh, uh, you know I can't go saying anything about that*. It'd spoil the surprise.

At the same time, I'd rub my tummy and lick my lips, hinting that whatever went into a bowl that empty would be out of this world.

To seal the deal, I'd mention that as a bonus, and for a limited time only, whoever bought this bowl would receive for absolutely free a bottle of the famous Ripp River Water, good for curing everything from squeaky bunions to loose teeth.

This was a bowl that ought to move fast!

In fact, I was in such a hurry to sell it that I snatched

it up to carry it out to the main channel. More fin traffic out there.

I figured that selling an empty bowl ought to prove once and for all that I didn't need to go back to school but was ready to hustle door-to-door.

That was how I discovered that the bowl really wasn't empty after all. It turned out to be filled with another year of classes at the Three-Berry Academy for the Totally Gifted.

How could I have missed the noose around it?

Gravy Drop-off

Us Drop-offs make most of our living from salvaging shipwrecks. Our lodge is dug into a riverbank overlooking the main channel so that we can dive straight to work whenever a boat goes down.

We pride ourselves on being fearless when it comes to barge lights, whirlpools, things that go whoosh in the night, and eyes that never blink but glow from the depths.

My whole clan swaggers around as if we hauled teapots off the Titanic. And who's to say we didn't?

All this is pretty rough on me, Gravy Drop-off, the youngest member of the last hatch. I've yet to have any adventures to call my own. And now, one day away from my first night at the Three-Berry Academy, my clan's laying it on especially thick, remembering the years they spent pinned to their seats by Quiet Quickthorn's roving eye.

My older cousin Ragweedna had recently graduated with honors from Three-Berry and was offering me about a thousand tips on how to survive school. At the very end she summed everything up this way, "Just be thankful you're a Drop-off. The first day there most of your classmates will be so scared they'll be scrambling around looking for a hole to stick their tails in."

"Not me," I promised.

I'm on the skinny side for a troll who's old enough to start school, and I have spent a good deal of my time proving I'm braver than everyone else. Right then my tail was in a sling because I'd strayed too close to a passing motorboat.

"Now Ragweedna," my mother scolded, "I'm sure you don't need to be badmouthing your little cousin's classmates. She's more than able to handle that on her own."

"I'll do my best," I vowed.

"Just trying to be helpful." Ragweedna shrugged. "You know that the first day I was at the Three-Berry the headmistress wrote a number on the blackboard and made everyone bob up and down to the surface until somebody named it."

"Oh Ragweedna," my mother snorted. "Now you know that never happened."

"Uh-huh."

"You're just making it up to scare your little cousin."

"I can bob," I protested, though neither of them heard me. They were too busy huffing and trying to talk over each other.

"Am not," Ragweedna insisted. "I'm just trying to prepare her. It's no joyride over to the Three-Berry."

"Oh, honestly," my mother said. "Gravy, don't you listen to a single word of what she's saying. Why if Quiet Quickthorn made everyone do that, her students would be bobbing up and down for years. Just ask your cousin if she can name a single number that ever got written on that blackboard. Go on. Ask."

"I sure can," Ragweedna proudly answered. "One."

"Oh one," my mother scoffed, shooing a sunfish away from the kitchen counter. "Ragweedna, you know, and I know, that Quiet Quickthorn isn't the kind of teacher to waste time with questions that everyone already knows the answer to. And you also know, or at least you better, that one is the only number that any troll in this entire valley knows. And I defy you to name a troll anywhere who has a wet tail and knows any number other than one. It's just not natural.

"And what's more, Quiet Quickthorn wouldn't know any number but one to write on that blackboard. She's a troll too, isn't she? So Gravy, don't go getting your snout all fizzed up about this nonsense. There won't be anybody expecting you to call out numbers over there, or bob to the surface until someone does."

"I knew that," I told them, though no one paid me much attention.

But later, when my mother paddled out of the room, Ragweedna couldn't resist whispering, "She'll try to make you spell too."

"Naw."

"Yes. You'll have to sniff some letters before you get out of there."

"Naw," I repeated, though deep down inside myself, somewhere between my first and second stomachs, I felt a little flutter, as if a centipede with cold feet was shuffling about.

But that wasn't anything compared to what my mother's sister Sweetcrest had to say when she popped by for a puffball recipe. She'd attended the Three-Berry too, and one look at me started her talking about the academy during the floods of '51, '52, and '53.

"Old Quiet-puss made everyone stay in their chairs through every one of them."

"Couldn't even go to the bathroom?"

"Only if you could get someone to hold onto your chair while you were gone. She didn't want any of the school's property swept away by the current."

"You're making that up," Mother chided, though of course she couldn't be absolutely sure because she hadn't gone to the Three-Berry herself.

"Uh-uh," Sweetcrest answered, sounding more like a kid than I had ever noticed before. "Snail up my snout, wiggle till I pout if I am."

"Oh you."

"We had to sit there the whole time," Sweetcrest insisted.

"That's just silly," my mother complained. "Don't go putting ideas like that in this girl's head. Gravy, don't you believe a word of what she's saying. Everyone knows that Quiet Quickthorn shuts that school down at the first sign of a flood. Your teacher may be a little crusty on the edges, but she's probably an old softy underneath."

"Soft as an anchor," Aunty Sweetcrest muttered. Raising her voice, she added, "All I can say is, be ready to hold on to your chair if there's any floods."

"She won't get me to stay in my chair if that happens," I predicted.

"She won't have to," Sweetcrest informed me. "That's why she keeps those huge snapping turtles around. I suppose you haven't heard about them either?"

"Snappers?" I tried not to gulp.

"Monsters."

"Enough!" Mother stomped her paw down. "You won't have to worry about those turtles a bit so long as you follow the rules. Now why don't we talk about something more pleasant?"

And so we did.

For the next hour we discussed the dredge that was deepening the channel up above Big Rock. It was uncovering some amazing stuff up there, old buggies, and a player piano that must have fallen off a steamboat, and a troll who'd been asleep for centuries, or so Sweetcrest claimed, and as soon as they woke her up, she wanted to know who'd stolen her pet clam whose name was Sherry-Ann.

When my mother went upstairs to the kitchen for the puffball recipe, Sweetcrest leaned close to me to whisper.

"Those snappers? If one of them clamps onto you, it won't let go until the river freezes over in the fall. And you better believe that old Quiet-puss consults with Echo Mudtoe every day to find out if there's any flood signs being reported—geese building up their nests, or carp retreating into the sloughs, or the lock and dam gates getting opened up all the way. Any of that and into your seats you'll be ordered. One or two of the 'fraidy-cats usually got tied right to their desks. But you being a Drop-off, she wouldn't dare go that far."

Shortly after that Grandpa Digger woke up over in a corner, took one look at me, and said, "I hear your whole school's gone soft. Way back when, before Quiet Quickthorn even had a schoolhouse to call her own and had to teach from a sunken rowboat, way back when she was still freckly behind the ears and felt like she had to prove something . . . way back then she made us sniff books till our snouts blistered. And don't go thinking it was anything we wanted to sniff either. History of snails or worse. The kind of stuff that can put you to sleep while standing up."

"Papa," my mother warned, "you used to tell me that exact same story."

"It was true then too."

"So why haven't I ever heard anyone else from that school tell it?"

"Code of secrecy," Grandpa said. "We all swore to never tell a living soul how rough that place was. Why do you know there was one time when she made us practice making our mark in mud till we wore our claws down to stubs? Couldn't even spear a dead minnow for months."

"Oh please."

"And that's not all either. There was another time she made us all sing."

"No." I cringed and grabbed for something to hold on to. Tails can be handy things.

"And all together too." Grandpa raised a paw as if testifying under oath. "All together at the same time. By the end of that song there wasn't a fish within miles. No lunch that day."

He might have kept rolling out horror stories too, if my great-grandmama hadn't arrived and announced, "That's nothing. Back when I went to that school, they called it Extra-Lumps Elementary. I'm talking way back before this Quiet Quickthorn had ever heard of the number one. The headmaster back in those days didn't go all gushy on you the way this new one does. Why, he kept a gang of crayfish in his desk who could cut you into fish bait if you so much as wiggled your tail out of turn. And I can tell you—"

"I think we've heard quite enough, thank you," my mother announced. And with that, she started pushing me out of the lodge, saying, "Gravy, maybe a little fresh water would do you some good."

But I dug in my claws and turned on everyone.

"You guys think you had it so rough," I said, "but you should have sniffed the letter my teacher sent me."

"Letter?" they all chimed in, shocked.

"When did that come?" My mother sounded suspicious.

"Yesterday. I could tell it was going to be bad even before I opened it. The envelope smelled all minty and fresh and terrible."

"You're making that up," cousin Ragweedna accused.

"Don't I wish."

"She never sent any of us a letter."

"She mentioned that." I nodded in agreement. "Said she felt as though she'd gone too easy on earlier classes but that she was putting an end to the free ride."

"High time," my aunt Sweetcrest declared. "Enough pampering."

"That's what she said," I told them. "She mentioned that she'd been thinking about running a tighter ship ever since of the floods of '51 and '52, when all her students had whimpered and cried until she got so tired of listening to them that she sent them home."

"Now just a minute—" Sweetcrest's tail started whipping back and forth so hard that it knocked a turtle off a couch.

"I complained about that back then," Grandpa Digger stated for the record.

"Yes," I went on. "She blamed her lapse on still feeling bad about taking it so easy on her students when she first took over the school. Back then she didn't have any idea what she was doing and went so far as to even bring pillows for them to sit on in that rowboat."

"What?" Grandpa squawked. "She never did any such thing."

"I remember those pillows," my great-grandmama spoke up. "You can bet we didn't have any such luxuries padding our bottoms back at old Extra-Lumps Elementary. They didn't spoil students in those days."

Everyone was muttering under their breaths by then, but I quieted them by saying, "Well, actually, her letter said she probably never would have used those pillows at all if they hadn't been left behind by the former schoolmaster, whose name was Lovey Dovey."

"Who?" Great-grandmama cried.

"Her letter said that at least she pulled out all the stitching on the pillows because they said things like *Hug an Eel* and *Kiss a carp*. But she later decided she shouldn't have used them at all and only did so out of respect for the former headmaster, though she did change the school's name. Extra-Kisses Elementary just seemed too soft."

"It was never called . . ."

"I'm going to go down there and . . ."

"Her tail's knotted up."

"Hold everything," my mother called out. "I want to hear what that letter said she had in mind for this year, if she's going to be so much stricter, I mean."

That got everyone's attention.

"Yah," they all growled.

"Let's hear what's going to be so tough."

"This ought to be good."

"Pillows! Bah."

Right about then was when I dove out the nearest window and swam for it. Of course there was no letter. Trolls didn't know how to write any more than they knew how to read.

Everyone was hot on my trail by then, gaining fast too, so when I spotted a baited snare dangling off the old wagon wheel bridge, I grabbed hold without even knowing what it was. I just wanted to be yanked beyond everyone's reach.

That's how I found myself hanging upside-down by my tail with a lawn sprinkler in my paws.

Down below, my entire clan was shaking their fists and threatening terrible things. They sounded awfully proud about how terrible.

Smuch Lipsmacker

Since I'm not doing anything but hanging upside-down from this tree, I might as well tell you my story, which is all about how I got tricked into going to that school again.

First off, my name is Smuch Lipsmacker, in case you were wondering who was telling you all this. And if you've heard anything about me from that Two Shellcruncher, don't believe a word of it. She's just jealous of anyone smarter than her, like me, especially since I'm a girl, like her.

Anyway, I wouldn't half mind swaying back and

forth here in the dark if my parents weren't so happy about it. That really gripes me.

You see, they've been after me to go back to the Three Berry Academy for the Totally Gifted ever since I came home for my summer break. One day into vacation and they were already asking me if I didn't miss my friends. As if I couldn't see through that excuse.

What friends?

That school, which is some kind of academy, is overflowing with clam-dips who couldn't swim their way out of a wading pool.

There's even one half-shell there named Drip Snipsnap who spends all his time slobbering over some lousy contraption he's trying to build. A bicycle—he calls it.

He's got some kind of seat on that thing that anyone with half a tail couldn't ever sit on. I dare you.

And it's got a curved rod of some sort that he calls its handlebars. He says they're used for steering, whatever that is.

I'm telling you, some of the so-called students at that academy should be planted over at Yellow Cat Bottoms, head down, if you know what I mean. They'd do just fine.

But my parents, they keep saying I'll get a chance to play some games and wouldn't that be fun? Like the time my classmates tied me to stump and left me for dead just as the sun came poking around. And why? For answering a question before anyone else—and I mean Two Shellcruncher—could.

About the only one who didn't get a hoot out of that stunt was dumb old Drip Snipsnap, and that was because he was all wrapped up in trying to figure out what something called a pedal did on that bicycle thing of his.

I bet I had to shout for half a day before he realized I was talking to him.

And close to another half day passed before he shut up about that pedal thing of his and untied my paws. It wasn't often that someone couldn't just walk away when he started talking about his bicycle, so he had me trapped. Brother, what a bunch of losers.

Don't try to tell that to my parents though. I tell you, the way they carry on about all the things supposedly taught at that school, you'd think nobody else along this entire river had ever figured out how to track turtles. To hear them tell it, my whole life's going to be miserable if I don't go back to that place and watch Two Shellcruncher wave her paw all over when the dried up old prune of a teacher asks one of her questions.

And I have to tell you, that old wart of a teacher never seems to run dry when it comes to questions.

I asked her one time if she was too lazy to look

up the answers. Was that the reason she was always lobbing her questions at us?

Boy, did things get quiet then. The whole classroom was lousy with it.

That old wreck of a teacher made me sit there with my tail in my mouth for the rest of the week. Little miss know-it-all Shellcruncher loved that, I can tell you.

The only one who didn't start mumbling as if he had his tail in his mouth was old Drip, and that was because he was so busy with something he called a chain, which was supposed to hook up to something called a gear, that somehow or other was supposed to power his bicycle if you stepped on it. He tried to show me once, but I just sat there without going anywhere.

He said that was because he only had one wheel for the thing, but that as soon as he found another wheel for it, I'd be zooming all over the place, faster than some locomotive, whatever that is. Personally, I don't think it'll ever replace swimming, but nobody listens to me.

Take my parents.

Lately they've been going on almost nonstop, and I mean all day and night, about how important it is for me to start learning all kinds of junk that I'll need to know when I get ancient, like them.

But when I ask them for one example, all they say

is stuff like troll history and river currents and what lousy beasties to stay away from.

I got so tired of listening to it all that I told them I was going on a swim. They said fine, it'd give me a chance to think about school and how it started tomorrow, which meant I'd be back with all my friends before I knew it, and enjoying all the terrific stunts we pull at school.

Wouldn't that be great?

I didn't have the strength to tell them what it's really like at the Three Berry Academy. How I don't have any friends because everyone's always saying I'm not any fun to be around because I act like I know more than they do, which isn't hard, terrible as they are at schoolwork.

They especially don't like me knowing more than that Two Shellcruncher.

I guess one smarty-tail is really all that any school has room for at any given time, and the position's already filled at the Three Berry because she's been there oodles of years longer than me.

What kind of a deal is that?

I tell you, I was ready to sign onto some leaky old boat full of smelly river pirates and forget all about school.

Maybe I would have too, if I hadn't noticed a bicycle wheel all tangled up in some tree's roots. I should have just swum right on by it, but seeing it reminded me of Drip Snipsnap trying to put that bicycle of his together and my heart went out to him. He was trying to make the best of a raw deal, and didn't I know it?

So I thought maybe I'd just drop this wheel off at his lodge, before I signed up with any pirate ships.

But wouldn't you know—that wheel was nothing but school bait. The instant I saw marshmallows stuck between its spokes I should have known something was wrong. And then a snare grabbed my tail and yanked me sky high.

What kind of luck is that?

At least I managed to hang onto the wheel for old Drip, who just might realize this year that I'm about the only friend he's got in that whole place. I hope so. Maybe school wouldn't be quite so bad if he did.

Happy Mudneck

I've been called Lonesome Mudneck for as long as I can remember. Everyone says I'm as lonesome as the river is long. You can ask anyone about that. Feel free. I'm telling you all that so you'll know that I meant it when I announced over supper, "I'm not going back to school if I can't take my friends."

My mother refused to take me seriously. "Now let's not be rash, dear. What would you do with yourself if you weren't in school? And eat the rest of your soufflé like a good little troll. You know how hard it is to get turtle eggs this time of year."

"But why can't I take my friends to school with

me?" I asked around a mouthful of boiled duckweed.

"Lonesome Mudneck, don't talk with your mouth full. It's unbecoming."

I swallowed before saying, "They wouldn't be any trouble."

"How could they be?" my mother asked. "I should think they'd never make it past snack time, hungry as those classmates of yours always look."

"Wouldn't teacher protect them?"

"I imagine she has her paws full with the students. They're not all angels like you, you know."

And she patted me on the snout, which almost always makes me crazy.

"But Mom, what will my pals do without me? Have you thought about that?"

"Heavens no. When would I possibly have time to do that?"

"I could sneak them inside my desk. No one would even know they were there."

"Loney," my mother chided, using that pet name of hers, "they wouldn't be happy in there."

"Why not? I could slip them little bits of pondweed and talk to them any time I took a book out."

"Now that's just silly. And I don't want to hear another word about it."

"But couldn't—"

"Not another word. I do believe it's time for you

to go outside and play. And while you're at it, you can say goodbye to your friends. Personally, I've heard quite enough about them."

Pushing off through the open front door, I was so mad that my tail curled up on me. My pals had been flitting around outside through the entire meal so had heard everything.

If a pumpkinseed can look sad, they were doing it, though for them it was something of an uphill struggle. You see, a pumpkinseed is a small sunfish with a cheery red dot on its side that always makes them look ready to burst into song, if fish can sing, and my friends can. That's what had drawn me to them in the first place.

Earlier that summer I'd been hanging around the front of our lodge one morning, after having been warned yet again what would happen if I wandered off, when this small school of half-dollar sized pumpkinseeds swam by in single file. Each one of them sang a single note from a song that scampered up and down the scales and made me tingle just to hear it.

My mother thought the neighborhood trolls were nothing but ruffians and brutes and worse, and she forbade me from playing with them. So when I saw the pumpkinseeds go gliding merrily past, I followed. Every now and then I even croaked out a bass note until they noticed me bringing up the rear and circled back to introduce themselves.

"Dasher."

"Dancer."

"Prancer."

"Vixen."

"Comet."

"Cupid."

"Donner."

"And Blitzen."

"And Rudolph."

"Where in the world did you get names like that?" I asked.

They laughed and said they had no idea, that it was just what their mother had called them. And then they'd asked what my name was.

"Lonesome," I'd said. "Lonesome Mudneck."

"Not anymore it's not," they'd all answered at once. "We're going to call you Happy."

And they did, and from that moment on I had the best summer I'd ever had, playing hide-and-seek in the willow roots, and name that cloud, and pin the eelgrass on the buffalo fish, along with a good deal of singing around any moon burst that lit up the bottom of the slough. But now all that was coming to an end.

"Come on guys," I said, moping toward the far side of the slough, "I guess this is—"

"Not so fast," Prancer interrupted. "What's that

up there?"

We all turned towards where he was pointing and saw a half-sunk bucket. It was bobbing in front of the willow tree without a care in the world. Little scraps of moonlight filtered through the willow leaves and bounced off the top of the bucket, making the water around it glimmer.

"Wait a minute," I said, brightening. "I think I know what that is."

"Tell us," the pumpkinseeds sang out in perfect harmony.

"Your ticket to school."

Without another word, I swam to the surface and discovered I was right. It was a minnow bucket. One that could protect eight pumpkinseeds from hungry students and at the same time had enough holes drilled in its sides for water to pass through and for them to see out.

Better yet, someone had looped a rope around it, giving me something to pull it by. I was just waving all my friends into the bucket when my mother called out, "Loney? What are you doing up there?"

"Nothing," I answered, though she may not have heard me, not as fast as that snare was whipping me and the bucket and all my pals inside the bucket out of the water.

"Wee!" we all sang.

First-grade Dripple

Don't call me First-grade Dripple. Them's fighting words. I'm in the next grade now. Have been for several years, and I don't have any plans on going back to first. No, ma'am.

Wild sturgeon couldn't pull me back there. Absolutely not.

I sat in first grade for so long that they gave it to me as my name. But that's all behind me now. I can tell the difference between minnows that are shiners and fatheads and rosewoods and diamondbacks, and I don't ever intend to ever go back. I've slaved too hard. No one could make me.

Well, almost no one.

Quiet Quickthorn has the power to send a student back. She's been known to do it too. Worse yet, she'd told me last spring, on the last day of school, that if I didn't quit giggling in class I was headed back to first grade.

"Of course the school's haunted," Quiet had lectured me when I tried to blame everything on a new ghost who had shown up. "Any student who drops out of Three-Berry has to come back after they're dead and finish their classwork no matter how long it takes. That's the guarantee I give parents when their student starts here. Everyone graduates—eventually. And believe you me, I wish everyone would stick with it the first time. There's no student harder to teach than a ghost. Always fading in and out, or moaning about homework. Never happy with the snacks either. But their parents knew what they getting into when they signed them up."

"But that ghost keeps tickling my tail," I told her.

"What do I tell you at the start of every year?" Quiet sternly asked.

"No excuses," I recited in a small voice.

"That's right. So you had better figure out a way to

deal with this, young lady, or I'll be sending you back to first grade, no wiggly ifs, ands, or buts about it. I won't have my classroom disrupted with your giggles. Am I understood?"

"Yes, ma'am."

Like anybody, I did my best to forget all that and enjoy my summer.

But now time's running out, and I've got to do something. That's why I paddled myself toward the head of Dead-end Slough and the rundown lodge that belonged to Till-death Slice-toe, who's a distant cousin on my father's side and is known as Aunt Tilly to family like me.

Aunt Tilly makes her living talking to the dead. Although everyone always complains that she charges an arm and a tail too much for her services, she's certainly never put any of her profits into her lodge. Geese had been known to mistake her roof for an abandoned nest, and she refuses to spend so much as a clam on freshening up her end of the slough. Normally that would have been fine with almost any river troll you can name. But there are limits! The water down there is so stagnant and dark that it feels like swimming through mud to reach her door.

And the large-mouth bass stationed on her stoop is about as lively as one mounted in your grandpa's den would be. In fact, he looks stuffed until you see him blink. Luckily, I was warned I'd need to bribe him with a night crawler to get past.

Inside, Aunt Tilly's lodge isn't much classier.

There's a single, cockeyed table with a black cloth draped over it. For a centerpiece, the table has the head of a moonfish, all bug-eyed and distant, resting on a lily pad. The head looks more alive than the bass guarding the door, until it blinks. Then you know that its pitch-black eyes can't see anything in this world, only the next.

As for Aunt Tilly herself, she had on her usual snake-skin shawl and so much half-baked clay jewelry that she jingled with every step. Her eyes were a mossy green. And smoky. She wasn't ever too happy with visitors who're still breathing either, especially if they're related to her. Relatives always want news from the dead for free.

"What is it?" she groused. "No, no, don't tell. I already know."

"You do?"

"Your great-great-grandfather already told me."

"But he's—" I bit my lip in time to stop myself from saying something stupid.

"Dead," Aunty Tilly finished for me. "So I hear you're trying to keep a spirit from tickling you during school. The best way to deal with something like that is to distract him. Can you get a picture of him while he was still alive?"

"I don't think so. I don't know who he was. "

"Pity. That'd be your best bet. A ghost generally loves to look at something from its past life. Fascinates them no end. Well, how about getting one of the ghost's relatives to sit with you? That might work, especially if it's someone he didn't get along with."

"But I don't know the ghost's name," I reminded her.

"Did you try asking? No, don't answer that. Of course you didn't. No one has any manners at all when it comes to the dead. All right then, I suggest you get something that a baby might like and set it on your desk. There's nothing that a ghost, especially a newly arrived one, hates more than being reminded of a baby who's all new and fresh to the world. Drives them loopy to think of it, especially how wonderful things used to smell. That's generally what they miss most, you know, the chance to sniff something. So if you put something on your desk that reminds them of what they've lost, the spirits will stay as far away from you as they can."

"I can do that," I said. Though after a moment, I added, "Ah, what kind of baby thing?"

"Whatever you can get your hands on. Human baby things generally work best. You know what a fuss they make about their newborns. Give me something hatched from an eggshell any day. But for your needs, I'd say a pacifier or teddy bear or one of those things they like to shake, ah, oh, just a second, what do they call those things?"

Aunt Tilly thumped her forehead with a knuckle until the fish at the center of the table opened its mouth and said in a surprisingly sweet voice, "Rattle?"

"That's it!" Tillie cried, snapping her fingers. "A rattle. You can't go wrong with one of those. If you want a sure bet, I'd say that's the way to go. Use a rattle to distract him."

"But where can I get one of those?"

"Gee," Tilly scoffed, "I wonder. How about from some human baby? That way it might smell like one too. Have you seen those little things drool?"

"But where would I find—"

"There's a whole town full of the nasty things right across the river. Now if you don't mind, I'm expecting a call from the Great Beyond that I don't want to miss. The rates go up after midnight, you know."

So I swam to a clump of arrowhead plants directly across from the river town of Blue Wing and settled in to wait. Gazing across the channel at the town, I found myself wondering yet again why humans tried to light up the night like day.

Maybe I'd learn something about that this year at school, though somehow I doubted it. That seemed more like an upper-grade kind of subject. Over in Blue Wing a bell chimed once, the way it did every night, sending a shiver through me 'cause I had even less of an idea why humans made so much noise.

And still I waited.

A barge churned by, and I settled in under water until it was well past. Next I heard a couple of humans talking in the levee park directly across from me. Too bad I couldn't make any sense of what they were saying.

"Don't let the cat out of the bag," one boy was pleading. "Not yet."

"Why not?" the other boy complained. "We can't keep it in there forever."

That made some sense, though why they'd bothered to put a cat in a bag in the first place had me scratching the tip of my tail.

But finally the two boys decided to go home and face the music, as they put it. What that had to do with stuffing some poor cat in a bag was far, far beyond me.

I crouched in the weeds and waited until the stillest part of the night drifted over the valley, sinking humans and their pets and any creature that wasn't magical so deeply into sleep that even a tugboat's foghorn would have only made them roll over and nuzzle their pillows.

Sure, a spell was behind all that, not that I cared.

I only knew that it was the one time of day that a troll like me could explore Blue Wing without someone shrieking E-E-E-E-E-K whenever I turned a corner.

Finally everything was so still that I couldn't make excuses any longer and started to town. I spotted a few other trolls making the rounds but kept to myself because I was so embarrassed about what I was doing. Stealing from a baby?

After peeking in the windows of a half-dozen houses, I figured out that any glass with a soft glow behind it was a good bet to be a nursery. Humans marked their baby's rooms with a tiny blue or red light.

I didn't have any trouble opening a window and getting inside either. Every first grader at the Three-Berry Academy has to learn a spell for that. Where everything fell apart on me was when I found myself beside the crib, gazing down at a sleeping human baby who had a rattle right beside it.

I just couldn't bring myself to swipe something from it. The baby looked so peaceful, even ugly as it was, with a round face and hardly any snout to speak of and smooth skin without so much as a shiny scale or freckle anywhere. And where was the thing's tail? How could I steal something from a creature so unfortunate as all that?

I couldn't even tell whether I was gaping down at

a boy or girl.

Though most trolls believed that humans color-coded their babies, I couldn't remember what pink meant.

And, well, when I finally did bring myself to pick up the rattle, its hollow, rustling sound made the baby stir and me freeze.

What if the stillest time of the night was ending? I didn't want to wake the thing. Not that I was scared, but I couldn't bear the thought of seeing its eyes open.

Everyone said human eyes weren't orange but brown, or even blue, a possibility I couldn't fathom at all. I didn't want the little thing to start crying either. Hard as it was to believe, I've heard that trolls could frighten humans.

How would I feel if someone crept into my room in the middle of the afternoon, while I was sound asleep, and stole something important to me, say a turtle shell or fish fin? I wouldn't be happy. Not at all. I'd be mad. My tail would crinkle. And if I woke up to find that human gazing down at me, I might have daymares forever.

All right. That did it. I'd decided. I wasn't going to take a rattle from anything so helpless as this. But that put me in a real snail shell too, because I knew I couldn't go back to the Three-Berry Academy without something to keep that ghost at bay.

A single giggle would send me back to first grade. If there was one thing for sure about Quiet Quickthorn, it was that she always kept her word. And that was when I made another even bigger decision.

"I'm dropping out," I told myself. "I don't care if I have to come back and haunt that school myself. She wouldn't dare make a ghost go back a grade, so I'll be all right."

That left me with more decisions to make.

If I tried going home and announcing I was done with school, I'd get chased straight to my desk by my own clan.

That wouldn't work.

I'd have to strike out on my own, which really left me only one place to go and that was the same place everyone ran away to—that mess of islands downstream from Blue Wing. There were supposed to be plenty of places to hide out down there if you didn't mind pirates and the way they carried on.

So I headed back to the river and dove in, floating on my back and gazing up at the stars blazing above as I let the current carry me to a new life. It was all going quite smoothly too, until I heard a small whimper from the far shore. Actually, it was coming from the clump of arrowhead leaves where I'd earlier hidden. I paddled over to investigate because it sounded as though someone was in trouble.

The closer I drew, the louder and unhappier the sound became until I waded into the plants and discovered a tiny human baby squalling. It was cradled in a basket that bobbed up and down on every little wavelet pushing through the bed of plants.

"How'd you get here?" I asked.

My question only made the infant cry all the harder and reach its pudgy little hands toward me as if wanting to be held.

"No way," I said, backing off. The infant's eyes were wide open and they weren't a proper, glowing orange at all.

Seeing me move away set the tyke off like a siren.

"Settle down, settle down," I pleaded, glancing about to see if there were any parents nearby. But nobody was in sight, so I did what any troll mother would have—scolded the baby, saying, "What's to worry about? You're out here on the river in the middle of the night with everything dark and darker. What else could you ask for?"

The baby didn't see it that way at all and fussed even louder.

It wasn't until the thing had to stop bawling to catch its breath that I heard another sound.

A faint rustling was coming from closer to shore, from beneath a cottonwood. Then the baby started screaming again, covering the sound up. Having heard enough from the infant, I clomped over toward where the rustling had come from, thinking that whatever I'd heard had seemed familiar.

That's how I found a baby rattle resting atop a broad arrowhead leaf.

"Is this what you need?" I asked over my shoulder.

The baby suddenly quieted and made a goo-gooing sound, as if saying yes.

"Must be," I reasoned. "Hold on."

Bending over, I picked up the rattle.

I never got a chance to return it to the baby though. The instant I touched it a snare grabbed my tail and yanked me high into the cottonwood, where I hung upside-down with a perfect view of the baby in the basket.

Except that the basket was fading out of sight before my very eyes. And the baby was disappearing with it. The rattle was real enough though. I even gave it a little shake at the baby who was quietly vanishing into the moonlight just as a cold, cold claw started tickling my tail, making me giggle.

One-bite Skeeterfog

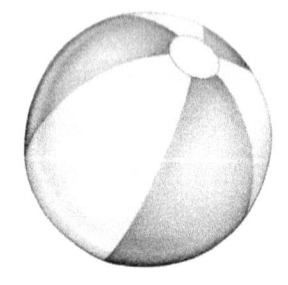

Nobody on the whole stinking river could agree on what the ball was supposed to be used for, or even why it had all those different slices of color.

Stewy Leechlicker claimed he's once seen humans playing catch with it on a beach.

Left-Righty Fishup wouldn't shut up about how it must have escaped from a ball museum.

Plunk Deepwater called it his uncle, who was under a spell. When he tried to understand what it was saying, I tried to tell him that nobody else could hear a thing. Do you think he'd listen?

Huff Junk tried to blow it away. He burst a cheek while puffing.

After trying to out-think it, Two Shellcruncher had to cool her brain off by dunking her head in the river. I wasn't the only one who offered to help her with that.

Wednesday Dropoff threw a leech at it.

Skinny Waddleton climbed out on a limb and sprinkled confetti over it.

All the trolls from Dogleg Slough fled.

A passing barge shined a spotlight on it, holding it there until rounding a bend.

Dawn aged it worse than a dry pickle.

A blue heron smacked into a cottonwood while trying to fly and keep an eye on it at the same time.

Three snails claimed they'd followed the evening star to it.

I bragged I could swallow it whole, but I never got a chance to follow through on that. The snare got me first. Me, One-bite Skeeterfog. I ask you—does that sound fair?

Burpetta Sludge

"I don't think I'm going to make it to school tomorrow."

That was me, Burpetta Sludge, moaning from my bedroom as if on my deathbed. I'd been laid low on the last night of summer vacation.

Fish lumps, I thought.

Or maybe slough droop.

I was too miserable to know for sure, but whichever it was, I had a chill. It could even have been a bad case of severe food poisoning. That rock-bass chowder we'd had for lunch had seemed a little too thick going down.

Poor me, lying in my nest of eelgrass as if somebody better toss me a lifeline quick.

"Who do you think you're kidding? You haven't been sick all summer. And now, on our last night of freedom, you all of a sudden can barely lift your head? Clam fuzz! Just a little bit ago you were feeling fine enough to play tag down by the sunken graveyard. So you can drop the act."

That was my older sister, Saintessa, looking in from the hallway. She was in charge while our mother was off to Tilldeath Slice-toe's place to have a word with our grandmother who'd had an argument with a barge and lost.

Indignant as Saintessa sounded, she must have been planning on being sick tonight too. That wouldn't do. Whenever we both came down with something at the same time, our mother knew. She just knew. And no matter how splotchy we played it, she packed us both off to school on general principle.

"Come on, Tessa," I pleaded. "Have a heart. You know what Quiet Quickthorn's like. If you dropped a match on the first night at the Three-Berry, the whole place would go up in smoke."

"Your school's underwater," Saintessa pointed out.

"Exactly."

"That doesn't even make sense. And why, I'm asking . . . WHY do you always get to be the one who's sick the first night?"

"Because I'm a sickly—" cough, cough, "—child who has to build up her strength."

"Foo-ha! You'll just get behind on your homework, which will only make you even more sick."

"That'd be terrible," I said, sounding hopeful.

"I'm not going to take this sitting down," Saintessa threatened.

"What are you going to do about it?"

"Go lie down in my room and start moaning. I think I just sprained my tail."

"While standing in the hallway?"

"Hey, it's a dangerous place."

"You do that," I predicted, "and we'll both get sent to school."

"What a pity."

"I'll make you a deal," I begged. "You give me the first week and I'll leave you the second."

"Now you need the whole first week?"

"I feel awfully poorly."

"Why you little—"

But just then our mother skimmed through the lodge's front door with a hearty, "I'm home."

Saintessa called out from the hallway, "How's Grandma?"

"Oh, fine," our mother loudly answered. "Sends

her love."

"Did she want something?" Saintessa asked, shooting me a knowing look.

Of course it didn't take a genius to figure out that our grandmother had wanted something. She'd sent word to Tilly Slice-toe, the local talker to the dead, that she needed a word with her daughter. Tilly had sent her big-mouth bass over with a note. I rolled my eyes to show that I'd known all that.

"Just to tell me that neither of you are sick," our mother sang out, "and that you can both go to school."

Saintessa wagged her tail at me, and crossed her eyes too, before leaving me alone to plot my next move.

The message from our granny didn't leave me many options, but I considered them carefully. I hadn't been kidding about the Three-Berry Academy catching fire if someone dropped a match on it. Quiet Quickthorn makes us all sit so stiff and straight that at times it felt as though even just thinking of a spark would set the whole school ablaze, even if it was underwater.

Still, at the start of every school year Quiet Quickthorn laid out the rules she expected us to follow. If I could finagle my way out of hearing all that, then I'd have an excuse when later on I broke some rule or other. I could claim I'd never heard about the rule.

Lowly I started groaning, letting one leak out every few minutes. There wasn't any hurry. I didn't want to overplay my hand. After all, there was always the chance that our mother would decide that my grandmother hadn't known what she was talking about. Granny often didn't.

Just because a troll was dead didn't make them some kind of expert.

And Granny was awfully far away, wasn't she? And her eyesight had been failing her even before she mistook that barge for a sandbar. So maybe she'd been mistaken about what she'd seen her granddaughters trying to pull.

Playing the sick card still seemed worth a shot.

For the next couple of hours I kept up the moaning, mixing in some expert groaning now and then. I worked it slowly while playing fetch with a muskrat who'd swam in through my bedroom window. There wasn't any hurry. I didn't need to be really sick until closer to school time. That's when it counted. Best to build up to it.

But then I heard voices at the front door and stopped moaning all together to listen. There were two or three voices, and I sensed they were talking about me. Finally my mother stuck her head into the hallway and called out, "You've got some friends to see you."

"Who?" I croaked, trying to sound weak and cold and stuffed up, but at the same time wanting to be heard.

"Oh, Mudd and Artum. They want you to come out and play. Why don't you? Supper's still a ways off. That rotting log's taking forever to cook. And besides, a change of scenery will probably do you some good."

"I'm not sure if I'm up to it," I feebly answered.

"They're talking about going over to the boat harbor and pulling out a few drain plugs," my mother cajoled.

Great! That was too much to bear. I had been after my pals all summer to yank out those plugs and sink some boats, and now that time was running out, and they had one night left—now they were finally getting around to it? They were trying to squeeze in one last hurrah before homework buried us alive, that's all.

Struggling to my feet, I limped down the hallway, holding my side and whispering through clenched teeth, "All right. I'll give it a try."

"You do that," my mother encouraged.

"But you might have to come get me. If I collapse or something."

Pitiful my sister mouthed at me from across the living room.

"I might not make it far," I warned my friends, both of whom knew my tricks well enough to promise they'd take it slow so that I could keep up.

We poked along until out of sight of my lodge,

stopping here and there so that I could rub my lower back or catch my breath. But as soon as we disappeared around the first bend I had a miraculous recovery. Imagine that. Opening up our strokes, we made time.

"Those boat plugs won't wait forever," I reminded them, leading the way.

"Our last chance," Artum agreed.

"Hold on," Mudd said. "What's that over there?"

We'd just left the water to take a shortcut across Poison Oak Island, and Mudd had spotted a faint bluish light off the path. He was always spotting something just off the path.

"Who cares?" I forged ahead.

But Artum joined Mudd for a look, which slowed me down.

"Could be something good," Mudd said.

I couldn't argue with him there. The week before had seen heavy rains, and the river had already risen and fallen, so maybe the waters had left something valuable behind.

But no, as we got closer, I could see that it was only a blue bottle from an old medicine show. They were common in troll lodges up and down the river. A shipment of them had long ago been scattered in a steamboat wreck. They were great for storing carp sauce and dried catfish whiskers and what have you.

Drawing closer, we saw that this particular bottle had never been opened, which explained why it gave off such a strong light.

The medicine inside those old bottles had been known to burn holes in rock and straighten out crooked claws.

Just a drop or two had been reported to restart stopped hearts.

A full bottle might actually be worth something at the store called Trolls & Things over in Big Rock. The old lady who ran that place had been known to pay serious clams for unopened bottles of old medicine.

But I didn't want anything to do with medicine bottles. If word ever got around that I'd traded in a bottle of it instead of used it myself, my mother would know for sure that I was faking it.

"I thought we were after boats," I complained.

My friends didn't let up though. Mudd was bending over to pick the bottle up.

"Hold it!" I blurted. "That thing could be booby-trapped. It's just the kind of bait that Quiet Quickthorn would put out for someone who's sick as much as me."

"Looks safe to me," Artum said.

"You say that every year just before we get caught."

"He does," Mudd agreed.

"So I say we give this thing a wide berth. It'll be

there on the way back if you're still interested."

With that, I stepped over the bottle and on to the log behind it, which was the one thing I shouldn't have done.

It appeared that my teacher had known that's exactly what I'd do. The snare closed around my tail the instant my foot touched the log. The cry of anguish I made while being pulled heavenward didn't sound fake or sickly at all.

Nor-I Brighteye

The walls of my bedroom are lined with the tongues of old boots and shoes. Sneakers too. Around sunset a current sweeps through my window and the tongues all wag up and down as if speaking.

Maybe that was why I barely bothered to talk. All those tongues did it for me.

Once or twice a year Quiet Quickthorn managed to coax a yes or no out of me, if she was lucky. Saying that much can tucker me out for months.

Tongue collectors often stopped by to admire my collection.

Chefs paid dearly for shavings off the oldest boot tongues, an essential ingredient in several holiday delicacies.

Until a snapping-turtle alarm system was installed, I'd had occasional trouble with theft.

If you wanted to see a tongue from an Oxford wingtip or a paratrooper's boot, my place was the spot. I had them all, even a tongue that had once belonged to the Great Two-Toe Gartooth, who was the first troll to settle our stretch of river and boasted that he'd cut the tongue from a rock troll's boot one dark, wild night. Old as that tongue looked, it didn't do much wagging.

One rainy night in late summer, I found a lovely old boot tongue, all mossy with age, on the bank above our lodge. Someone had dropped it right out in the open, atop a river cabbage leaf.

I didn't utter a word, just admired it for a while, and then, knowing it'd been left there for me, I collected it and waited to be whipped upward by my tail. I'd been caught the same way for so many years that Quiet Quickthorn didn't even bother sprinkling so much as a single marshmallow on the bait. I never could resist adding another tongue to my collection.

The Old Man

Around dusk I liked to turn the rocking chair on the front porch of my fishing shack toward the river. I sat there through the night then, watching a cowgirl hat that someone had set on the riverbank.

Every year the same thing happened on this night. Never mind the date. That's for me to know. Sometime in late summer, that's all I'm saying. I had it marked on my calendar so that I wouldn't miss it. The night of the hat.

It was never the same kind of hat. Over the years

I'd seen stocking caps, baseball caps, pith helmets, nurse's caps, football helmets, porkpie hats, policemen's hats, sailor's caps . . . a long list, all set on the riverbank in front of my fishing shack. I was an old man who had lived along the river a long, long time, and I'd seen enough hats to fill a haberdashery.

This year a red cowgirl's cap had appeared. Small as it was, I figured it must have belonged to a kid.

Around the hat, same as every year, was a loop of yellow nylon rope.

How the hat and rope got there, I'd never seen, for it always happened when I dozed off. For years I'd tried to catch who put it out, but now in my old age, I didn't worry about it so much anymore. At some point there'd be a splash, and I'd wake up to find this year's hat and rope in place.

Of all the strange things that happened along this stretch of the Mississippi, this had to be my favorite. I guess that's why I never told anyone else about it either. It was a secret I liked to keep to myself. I enjoyed it more that way. Knowing about it made me feel closer to the river. And besides, who'd believe me? I was just a crazy old fisherman who lived by too much water.

Now I sat in my rocker and waited.

Eventually river trolls would creep up the riverbank to gaze at the hat as if they couldn't quite believe what they were seeing.

They're secretive creatures, river trolls. I'd rarely caught glimpses of them over the years, and then only out of the corner of my eye as one of them dove into the river or jumped behind a tree. They're pretty darn quick and don't make much of a splash for such big creatures.

Sometimes I saw a line of bubbles working its way toward my rowboat when I was out fishing. They would come at me in a straight line, disappear under the boat, and reappear on the other side.

Somewhere in there my fishing line was sure to snap.

And whenever any of the bubbles popped on the surface I almost thought I heard laughter. Experience had taught me to give up fishing for that day. I'd only keep losing line and tackle.

So I sat on my creaky old porch, waiting for the stillest time of the night, when only rivery things are free to roam. Finally, when I was almost asleep, a small troll, a girl I thought, crept completely out of the river as if the hat was calling to her. She was holding a stick. They did that sometimes. Not that it ever did them any good.

What happened next made me want to do something to help them. They always crouched there shivering in the moonlight or starlight or gloom (depending on the year), all the while acting as though wishing they had the strength to turn around and leave.

But they never did. The hat called too strongly to them.

They weren't the only ones who'd lost all their strength by then. When I'd been much younger, I'd always tried to help the trolls out by shouting a warning, something like *Go Back!* Or *Don't try it!* But my mouth had always been too weak to form the words. I guess I was under a fleeting kind of spell that had the entire riverbank in its grasp. All a non-troll could do was watch.

In time one of the trolls would reach for the hat. Some grabbed at it as fast as they could, as if planning to make a run for it. Others tried to spear it with the tip of a stick so that they didn't have reach over the rope around it. A few rigged up a vine on an overhead branch and tried to snatch the hat as they swung over it.

No go.

The results were always the same. The rope snare protecting the hat would latch onto their tails and whip them up into the tree above them. There they hung upside down, gazing forlornly at the hat below them.

When morning light started to arrive, I regained enough strength to do something. I'd once tried freeing a caught troll, but it had snarled and snapped so fiercely that I'd never tried that again.

Instead I settled on giving each troll the hat they'd been after. I held it out to them on a stick.

I also speared an apple and held that out to them too. They looked awfully hungry hanging from that tree, so it seemed the least I could do.

The strange thing was—once they had the apple in their paws, not one of them ever took a single bite of it. No, they breathed on it, and polished it on their chests as if planning on giving it to someone. They made those apples gleam!

I never managed to stay awake long enough to see what happened next. My all-night vigil left me too tired. All I knew was that when daylight finally woke me I always found myself alone.

Dimwhittle Wetwater

The news spread up and down the river throughout the night. I suppose the moths arrived first of course. They usually do, drawn by the singing. That birthday candle had a low, damp voice that sang a slow song with only two words to it.

Cherries jubilee. Cherries jubilee. Cher-ries ju-bi-lee.

A few moth old-timers, who'd become hard of hearing, flew into the flame to hear the song better, but younger moths only spiraled around the candle until they'd memorized the words. From there they flew off to sing it elsewhere.

Except for mayflies, nobody else but moths could hear a candle sing, and all the mayflies I've known said they only caught little bits and pieces that sounded sort of like tulips waking in the spring, if you've ever been lucky enough to hear that. But all that didn't matter too much this time because the mayflies were done for the summer, so like I said, it was only the moths who flocked to the song.

Naturally all the fluttering of moth wings drew others toward the candle. Emerald beetles and crickets and groggy grasshoppers came skimming and hopping and gliding through the tall grass along the riverbank. Watching them made me smile.

Fox and mink and muskrat caught the scent of the candle and worked their way toward it too. I knew one of the foxes. He lived in a culvert that went nowhere, that one by the wing dam with the frog statue on top of it.

A mother deer led her fawn toward the candle. I'd been wondering why I hadn't seen her around.

In the water, turtle heads bobbed to the surface like they will. Small bluegills and sunfish peeked out from beneath the turtles' flippers. Everybody always gets all buddy-buddy when a candle gets lit.

Up above, nighthawks dove toward the flickering candle, pulling up at the last second because the flame wasn't what they'd been expecting. The fanning of their wings caused the candle's flame to gutter, as if about to go out, and we all held our breath until it straightened and flared slightly brighter.

Far above, the face of a small boy was pressed against the window of a jetliner passing by high overhead. I waved but he was too far away to see me.

Beyond the boy, stars twinkled their support for the candle.

We river trolls arrived last. Me, Dimwhittle Wetwater, got there before any other trolls, of course. One of us Wetwaters always do. Some of the others, who got there right after me, started egging each other on almost at once.

"Would you look at the size of that blaze?"

"The size of a blaze doesn't matter," I told him.

"The last troll who tried touching one of those things smelled like Oh-Oh Logrot's campfire for years."

"That's 'cause he tried swallowing it," I explained.

"A fire like that? Had he been in the nettles?"

Just then the flame flickered and we all jumped back, only to creep forward again when it got steady.

"There ain't one of you experienced enough to handle a conflagration like this and don't even pretend you are," I warned them.

"What? Do we look crazy?"

"Don't pretend you weren't thinking it," I lectured. "Just don't."

"So what if we did?" one of them lipped off. "It ain't no scales off your tail, Dimwhittle."

"Oh yeah?" I sassed right back. "Well I know how this works. Tomorrow you'll be bragging all over the backwaters that you put out the blaze before it turned the whole river into steam."

"That little flame?"

"Little my foot. I'm surprised Blue Wing hasn't sent every fire truck they own out here."

"Stand back all of you," a newcomer announced. "I'll take care of this."

"Hardy-har-har."

"Maybe I should use your nose to snuff it out."

"You and whose army?"

And while all that tough talk was going on, I decided that I couldn't stand another second of such blinding brightness. But turning my back to the candle and swimming away wasn't an option either. I'd already seen the flame, so now it was in my head, and I couldn't very well hose it down in there. So if I was going to get any peace, I'd have to see it put out. That was the only way it'd be out in my head too.

Summoning all my courage, I stepped around everyone who was arguing and plucked up the candle to pitch it into the river. Instead, the snare that no one had noiced in all the excitement closed around my tail and zoomed me upwards.

Surprised, I dropped the candle.

It landed in the crowd of trolls, who screeched and danced until one of them accidentally stamped it out.

At least that put out the flame in my head too. Thank goodness. After having seen a wildfire like that? It was kind of soothing to sway upside down in the dark.

Steamalita Willowbug

When Steamalita Willowbug made up her mind to quit school, nobody bothered trying to talk her out of it.

How do I know?

Because that's me. I'm her, Steamalita Willowbug, and when I make up my mind, nothing—not tugboats or flying catfish or chiggers—can change it.

That teacher what's-her name, down at that Three-Berry Academy place, she works her students too hard. I like to take my time, relax, not hurry. Why hurry? I was a big river troll, even for the Willowbugs, and it took time to get my tail warmed up.

And my brain needed a good half hour of rest in between thoughts, especially if I was tackling something new, and that what's-her-name down at the Three-Berry was always diving into something new. At least once a week it happened. Without warning. No, I'd had enough schooling.

"Oh you have, have you?" my mother said. "So just what are you going to do with yourself?"

Great. I hadn't thought that far ahead. Why should I have to do anything with myself? But I didn't get a chance to ask that one. My mother wasn't done talking. In fact, she seemed to just be getting started.

"Because one thing you're not going to do, young lady, is sit around here all day collecting silt. That's not in the cards. You're what, fifty some years old now? Or is it seventy? Whatever, you're a little young to be dropping out of school, if you ask me, but judging from the way your report cards smell, you haven't been doing anything but sleep over there anyway. So maybe it is time for you to get a job and start contributing something around here. You won't be the first Willowbug to finish your studies after you're dead."

Studies after I died? I'd forgotten about the Three-Berry's famous everyone-graduates guarantee, but being dead was so far away that I quickly decided to forget about it again.

But a job? Me, I didn't much care for the sound of that.

A job might require a little more work than I'd been planning on. I'd heard grownups complain about jobs and had been hoping to put off getting one for as long as possible.

With any luck, forever.

I had a great uncle Runaway who didn't do much of anything but lay around his hole all day. At clan gatherings all he did was yawn and say please pass the muck biscuits. Maybe I could get a job like he had, though I wasn't quite sure what a bum did. I'd managed to sleep through any talk about careers at school. Despite what's-her-name's best efforts, I did manage to catch a few winks now and then.

But my mother smashed my plan to be a bum before I could even get comfortable with it.

"And if you think," my mother lectured, "that I'm going to let you turn into another Runaway Willowbug, forget it. One freeloader is about all this clan can support. Not going to school? Fine. Good. You tell me what your job's going to be, and I'll pack roasted clams for your midnight snack. Otherwise—school. And that means you've got one day to find a job, and no I'll-find-one-later business. If I hear the slightest hint of that, I'll haul you down to the Three-Berry myself. Remember how well that went last year? And that was nothing compared to the show I'll give them this yer. So if you think . . ."

By which point I had heard enough and retired to my room, regretting that I'd ever bothered getting out of bed that afternoon. That's what I got for being reckless and rolling out before dark.

So, a job. Me, I didn't have any idea of how you went about getting one those things. What talk I'd heard about it hinted that a job might be harder to catch than a cold.

Gradually, I remembered that Echo Mudtoe, the river crier, called out job openings when she went by at night. Not that I had ever paid attention to any of that before, but if it would spare me from having to start the grade that came after the first one all over again, I guessed it might be worth a listen, even if I had to hurry.

I made it down to the mouth of the Blue Mist Slough in time to catch the tail end of Echo's evening announcements. The crier had a high, scratchy voice whose breathlessness made everything sound urgent as your tail catching fire. Normally, I stayed as far away from her as possible.

". . . washing. Stolen." Echo ended each item by loudly repeating its most important part. "Stolen!" After a pause, she then launched into her next bit of news. "The Lipsmacker clan offers a ten clam reward for information leading to the return of their pet turtle Speedo . . . Reward! . . . The Snipsnaps invite you to an egg hatch potluck on the night of the waxing quarter moon. Refreshments provided . . . Egg hatch! . . . Yellow Cat Bottoms has been awarded the Most Picturesque Bottoms award of the season . . . Award! .

"Moving on to job openings! Job Openings! Ragweed Enterprises seeks experienced star-grass weaver. Full benefits. Chance to advance. Apply in person . . . Ragweed Enterprises, star-grass weaver. . . . Yellow Cat Bottoms seeks mucker-outer. Bucket provided. Apply in person . . . Yellow Cat Bottoms, mucker-outer . . . Gnome Gardens West seeks night watchtroll. Excellent beginning job. Minimum duties. Start tonight! Apply in person . . . Gnome Gardens West, watchtroll . . .

"Darkness forecast provided by Smokeclam Stainers, the trolls who can stain anything you want, no job too big or small. Contact Tarbrush Smokeclam for free samples. And now the forecast—starlight till ten, half moon to . . ." Her voice trailed off, heading toward the next slough over.

Me, I had heard enough and didn't follow. I turned downstream instead, hoping to land a job as a night watchtroll. The part about minimum duties had caught my attention.

I didn't need any directions to find Gnome Gardens West. Any river troll who'd ever been hungry knew where that place was. If you had a hankering for tomatoes or celery or strawberries or anything that gnomes grew in their gardens, then you'd raided it before.

While I crossed the main channel and skirted the early evening lights of Blue Wing, I tried to recall the last time I'd been to Gnome Gardens West. I thought maybe I'd been after a cucumber that trip, though it could have been asparagus, but I was sure about one thing—I'd been chased by the night watchtroll, an old gimp who claimed to have lost the tip of his tail in the goblin wars.

I'd never heard of him catching anyone, not even during watermelon season and those suckers were big to carry, just the right size for blocking chimneys. The old watchtroll had been so far out of shape that I had gotten my cucumber or asparagus without having to run more than ten steps.

Too bad that whichever vegetable I'd grabbed had been disgustingly sweet and crunchy and grubless. Not what I'd been craving at all. That'd been years ago, and it'd left such a nasty taste in my mouth that I hadn't bothered going back since. Too much work.

Gnome Gardens West covered a couple of sandy acres upstream from Blue Wing on a marshy little jut of land. A rotted out wooden dock that was missing most of its planks and half its posts marked the spot.

I had barely planted one paw on the beach next to the dock than huge truck headlights that were higher than my snout flashed on, catching me half in and half out of the river. A gruff voice behind the lights spoke through a megaphone.

"Stand right where you are! Don't twitch a tail or I'll run you over."

That didn't seem likely unless he was driving some kind of amphibian on wheels, but I wasn't taking any chances. I stayed put as the voice continued.

"State your business."

"I heard you were looking for a night watchtroll," I answered.

"So what if we are?"

"I'd like to apply. I guess."

There was some rough whispering away from the megaphone. That was followed by a suspicious question.

"Ever been here before?"

"Maybe."

"Told you," a woman's voice triumphantly declared, though she wasn't anywhere near as loud. No megaphone for her.

"What'd you expect?" the man answered, about half as loud as before because he wasn't speaking directly into the megaphone. "And besides, at least she'll know where to look for thieves."

"But how can we trust her?"

"How about we make her swear on her mother's grave."

"And what if she doesn't have a mother's grave to swear on?"

"What do you mean doesn't have a mother? How can she be here if she doesn't have a mother?"

"I mean," the woman blustered, "what if her mother doesn't have a grave yet? What if she's still alive?"

"So much the better," the man countered. "Do you think she'd want to put her own mother in an early grave by breaking her word?"

"You needn't be so high-and-mighty about it, Vladimir Buckthorn. It seemed a sensible point to me."

"And sensibly answered, Colette Jewelweed. Now do you mind if we get on with this? I heard some slugs galloping around the cauliflower last night, and I'd like to pay them a visit before they grow beards."

"Your visit sounds a little late to me," the woman huffed. "If they're already galloping, I mean."

"Yes, your majesty. No, your majesty. I'd rather be hoeing a row, your majes—"

That singsongy taunt ended with a squeal, as if one of his toes had been stomped on. A moment later, he got back on the megaphone in a hairy, dark mood.

"Will you swear to keep your paws off the produce?"

"I will," I answered, thinking that it easily beat going back to school, especially if it was cucumbers that were in season.

"On your mother's grave?" the woman prodded.

"On my mother's grave. When she gets one."

Just to be on the safe side, they made me repeat it all together.

"And do you promise to keep everyone else's paws off the produce too? Particularly the leafy greens?"

They sent me back to my mother's grave for that one too, but in the end they were satisfied.

"You're hired," the man growled, flicking off the headlights.

The man and the woman then climbed out of the truck and stepped forward, looking like every other gnome that I had ever seen gathering wild berries and marsh marigolds and willow bark. The man wore one of those traditional gnome hats, red and conical and half as tall as he was. The woman had a red hat that was square up top, so she seemed shorter, though they both topped off around my knees.

He, beard.

She, pigtails.

Red spots covered their cheeks. Gnomes are

known for getting overheated quickly.

"Got a name?" the man asked.

"Yup," I answered, not exactly used to job interviews.

"Goodness," the woman tsked.

"Leave it to me," the man assured her, as if he was used to dealing with trolls. To me he impatiently said, "So tell us your name."

"Steamalita Pipeton Toepaint Wigglewaggle Chirp-ache Ribbonknot Pop-pop Willowbug," I recited, giving my whole name because I wasn't sure what part of it they wanted. A river troll's name never stops growing, just like our tails, though as we age, both grow much more slowly.

"Any relation to Runaway Willowbug?" the man asked.

"A niece."

"No discounts for him," the man cautioned.

"He's not around," I told them. "Moved down below Five Creeks."

"Ran him out of the lodge, huh?" the gnome said, sounding as though he could have predicted it. "You lazy too? No, don't bother answering that. Every troll who applies for this job hasn't had any more get-up-and-go than a Brussels sprout. We'll take care of that for you. Here, you'll need one of these."

He handed me a long-handled hoe that he plucked

from out of nowhere.

"And one of these."

He pushed a misting bottle at me.

"And two of these," the woman added, dropping a pair of bags with shoulder straps at my feet. "Since it's your first night, we'll start you out slow, but don't expect us to go easy forever."

"And you might need this," the man continued, holding out a pruning hook. "This too." He leaned a square-nosed shovel against my knees.

"We leaving anything out?" the woman asked, eyeing up all the gear.

"No, that ought to do it," the man judged. To me he concluded, "You can eat all the bugs, slugs, and red centipedes you want. Free. No charge. Perk of the job. But all dirt remains in the garden. And the ladybugs are off limits. Am I understood?"

"Loud and clear," I reported.

"We've had ladybug issues before and we won't stand for it," the woman cautioned.

"No ladybugs," I repeated, stooping under the load they'd piled on me. "But if you don't mind my asking, what am I supposed to do with all this stuff?"

They thought that was about the funniest thing they'd ever heard and guffawed so hard they had to hold each other up so that they didn't fall over.

"Why, help keep this garden in order," the man

managed to say after he'd finally stopped chuckling. "You didn't think you'd just be sitting around on your tail waiting for carrot thieves to show up, did you?"

"That'd be a waste of good gardening time," the woman informed me.

"We're going to teach you how to weed and prune and mist and collect," the man explained. "All for free. There's universities would charge you a small fortune for what you'll learn here."

"We're going to make a gardener out of you." The woman sounded almost teary-eyed at the thought of it.

"What do you think of that?" The man hitched his thumbs under his suspenders and proudly thrust out his gut.

I considered dropping everything in my arms and making a run—not a walk—for the river. But that was the way back to school, and I couldn't bring myself to do it.

"Same as the others," the woman observed. "Speechless."

"Overcome with gratitude," the man said.

"Well, we've got a garden to tend," the woman stated, tugging on some gloves. "Weeds and pests wait for no gnome."

"Ay-yup," the man seconded. "One last thing though. Your previous trips over here, we'll just deduct them from your first paycheck. Any objections? No? Good. Why don't you start on that row of beets over there? Shake the dirt off good and don't mangle the tops. There's people who'll pay top dollar for those tops."

And so it started.

I had never known a night could be so long.

And while the night stretched on and on and on like some river that would never end because it didn't know where it was going, I could hear the two gnomes all over the garden, bossing plants around, and chasing off raccoons, and returning about every five minutes to check on how I was doing with the beets. They offered plenty of advice on how I might do better too.

There was but one river troll who tried sneaking into the garden that night, and the woman ran him off with her hoe before I even knew he'd dropped by for a spud.

False dawn had never smelled sweeter, a kind of heady brew of duckweed and river mist. By then I'd discovered that the only safe place to hide from the gnomes for a few minutes rest was the corn. Its stalks were tall enough to conceal me, though if I moved at all, the rustling sound gave me away. When that happened, one of the gnomes shouted from wherever he or she was that beets didn't grow that high.

Dawn was in full glory when the gnomes announced the day shift had finally arrived.

"You didn't exactly earn your keep," the man told me, checking my collection bags, which were mostly empty, "so we'll call it a wash. We won't charge you for what we taught you—"

"—or for that half a cucumber you ate," the woman interrupted.

"—and you won't charge us for your time."

"You'll have to get quicker at everything if you expect us to keep you around," the woman advised. "But if you're willing to try again tomorrow night, I guess we'll give you one more chance. It's not exactly as though we've got a bumper crop of candidates to choose from."

"Go on home now," the man urged. "The tools stay though."

"And don't try pocketing anything on the way out. We'll be keeping an eye on you. And by the way, that row of Yukon Golds you're standing in, way at the end there, you missed a weed. Why don't you pull that up on your way out? Any job worth doing is worth doing right, eh? But don't go expecting us to treat you so easy tomorrow night."

"Wouldn't be right if we did," the man agreed.

So I dragged myself down the row of Yukon Gold potatoes. It took the last of my strength to tug up the weed at the end of the row. I almost keeled over doing it.

Every bone in my body ached. Some ached twice.

Every joint creaked worse than a ghost ship in icy waters.

Every muscle sagged.

My tail felt brittle, as if about to shatter. Maybe it already had. I was too exhausted to cry and way too exhausted to point out that whoever had missed that last weed hadn't been me. I'd been working the beets.

Somehow I made it to the riverbank, but no farther, for there at the very end of the Yukon Golds, resting on the freshly tilled earth, was a lovely, fluffy pillow just waiting for me. I had one final thought before collapsing upon it.

No beets!

I was sound asleep before the snare around that pillow even had a chance to close around my tail and pull me into the river. The water barely woke me. The pillow stuck to the side of my snout thanks to a generous helping of marshmallows.

The last thing I heard before nodding off again was one of the gnomes saying disgustedly, "Would you look at that? Typical. Just typical."

Arithmetic Icksome

"Under no condition, young lady, are you to go anywhere near that school."

"Your father's right. We won't put up with it for another year. We've had enough of that place. If you think we enjoy hearing all the rubbish that teacher is filling your head with, well, forget it."

"Yah. Who said you could learn how to track turtles? I didn't learn about that until I was at least twice your age."

"Or talk to crows?"

"Or weave eel-grass?"

"Or makes friends with a Shellcruncher? If your grandfather hears about that, he'll rise up out of the river and throw mud at the moon."

"Your mother's absolutely right. Pretty soon you'll be telling us you're pals with a Brighteye or Dimwater."

"Oh honey, not that, please."

"And don't think we care if you have to go back and finish up after you're dead."

"That's right. With any luck we'll be long gone by then ourselves and won't have to hear about any of it."

"And don't go thinking we appreciate the way you come home acting so high and mighty just because they taught you something that we never even heard of when we were at school. Why for a cracked clamshell I'd go down to that place and tell your teacher just what I think of her academy. And that's another thing! Why can't she just call it a school? What's all this academy stuff?"

"Gifted? Ha!"

"No dear, you've got that wrong. You're supposed to say *Totally Gifted.*"

"I've never heard of such claptrap. I'm thinking it's high time we just got you a job. The turtle-shell factory is supposed to be hiring scrubbers. That might be just about perfect for someone who thinks she knows so much. It might actually bring you down a peg or two."

"About time, I'd say."

"Wait a minute. Just where do you think you're going, young lady?"

"Come back here this instant."

"You heard me."

"Shhh. What's she doing?"

"Going outside."

There followed a minute of silence, after which my mother and father crept over to our lodge's front windows to peek outside. Though they whispered, I could hear every word.

"Too thick?"

"Hardly."

"I just hope she bought it. She needs to be at school."

"You can say that again. For all our sakes."

"Hey, look!"

"I think she's going for it."

"She is. She is."

"Isn't that the same pencil that got her last year?"

"Sure looks like it. Same orange and everything."

"Hey! Is she sticking her tongue out at us?"

"Why that little . . ."

"Here comes the noose!"

"Hallelujah!"

"Yah, there she goes. But how are we going to get

her to that school next year?"

"We can only hope the good river will provide, dear. The good river will provide."

Nibble Nettleburst

I've been perfecting my foam recipes for years. My foam soups are to die for, and I 've made a small fortune on my foamy marsh juices, which have a reputation for sticking to your whiskers for weeks. My foam soufflé has been a blue-ribbon winner every time, with a recipe that has been made public by order of the king.

FOAM SOUFFLÉ

A cup of frog eggs
A mouthful of culvert water
A generous pinch of good old-fashioned dirt
A crumbled leaf of poison ivy
A fist full of crushed cockleburs

Mix in an old hubcap, marsh salt to taste, cook under full moon, serve on week-old lily pads.

And my foam pies have been banned 'most everywhere because of the scandalous ingredients.

FOAM PIES

Fresh fruit (Who cares what kind?)
Potato peels begged from passing barges
A puff of air from the valve stem of a truck
A box of laundry detergent (don't skimp)

Combine ingredients in bottom of leakyboat, stirring with an unlicked oil dipstick. Pour into old boots and bake on hot rocks for three July days.

In short, if an expert on foam was ever needed, the

call always went out to me, Nibble Nettleburst.

So I staggered backwards the instant I saw that glittering mound of foam heaped on top one of those beach balls that are always floating around.

Spotting a thin lariat surrounding it didn't slow me down a bit. It was love at first sight.

I swore I'd never seen such a delicacy before, and once I regained my footing, I licked that beach ball clean without even bothering to strap on my eating googles. Fast as that lariat was tugging on my tail? I didn't have time to bother with anything else.

Iffy Fishfly

My name's Iffy, not Spiffy, so don't think you'll get a rise out of me with that one. Heard it before.

But you're right about one thing. Iffy Fishfly really does hate mistakes, especially my own. I tell you, even a tiny flub can drive me wild! Sometimes I see spots. Other times I can feel a mistake coming on way before I even know what it will be. A tingle behind my ears gives it away.

That's why I don't want to go back to the

Three-Berry Academy. School is nothing but one chance after another to make mistakes. And in front of a classroom full of trolls too. The thought of it almost crumbles my tail to pieces. At least if I waited until I was dead to finish school I wouldn't know the other students.

"I think maybe I should stay home and help you this year, Mom. The caterpillars are looking extra furry this fall."

That was true. Everyone was predicting an early snowfall, followed by a harsh winter, and my mother wasn't getting any younger. Always stiff in the joints and a bit more drafty between the ears was how she put it. She needed help. Mine.

"That's sweet, Iffy. But a troll your age needs to be in school. I'll be just fine."

"What if you get iced in while I'm gone?"

"Your uncle Stump's right next door and has an ax. And if that fails, I'll just have to wait for a thaw. Everything will be fine. There isn't something else worrying you, is there?"

"No, no. Nothing at all."

"Because I know that sometimes you fuss about, well, things."

"Mom," I warned, realizing that it'd been a mistake to bring it up. I shouldn't have said anything at all, just stayed home and helped. That would have been the smarter move.

"You worry too much," she mothered. "That's all I'm saying."

"I just don't like to think of you here all by yourself, Ma. That's all I'm saying."

"Oh I'll hardly be alone. You know that someone's always dropping by to see me. Some days I can hardly find a minute to myself."

That was true enough. Someone was always visiting my mother. She had more friends than anyone I knew, unless it was my Grandfather Who-do.

Now there was a troll with connections. Everyone liked to be around him. He had a way of saying just the right thing to make you feel better. As a matter of fact, I decided to pay him a visit to ask what I should do about school. I came up with that idea right after promising Ma that I'd quit worrying, which was another mistake because it left me wondering how I'd ever live up to a promise that ridiculous.

To get away from all those worries, I pushed off for my grandfather's lodge. I might have made it there too, if I hadn't started wondering if possibly it wasn't a huge mistake to barge in on the old troll, who was after all a terribly important mover and shaker with a dozen incredibly river-stirring deals going on at once, any one of which was probably far more important than some grandson trying to worm his way out of going back to school because he was afraid of making a mistake.

That rather long thought slowed me down.

Floating up to the surface, I flipped onto my back to gaze up at the stars. As I drifted along, I was unable to shake the feeling that everything in the world was nothing but one gigantic mistake that I was somehow responsible for. I never bothered with trying to figure out how I could have ever done something so colossal. I just knew that when it came to mistakes, I've pulled off some lulus. That's how my uncle Duckwad found me, sniveling atop the slough.

"What now?" Duckwad said, barging in on my miseries. He was a well-known bully along the river and never bothered tiptoeing around anyone's feelings.

"Oh, nothing."

"Don't give me that crud. I've seen you moping around like this before. I'd be happy to box your ears if that'll help any."

"No thanks."

"Got any minnows?"

I dug into a pocket and handed several over without complaint. The only reason I carried candied minnows around in the first place was in case I ran into my uncle Duckwad. It would have been a painful mistake not to.

"That all?" Duckwad complained.

I tugged out my pockets to show I wasn't holding anything back.

"Next time you better have more. Aren't you supposed to be in school?"

"Not yet."

"You don't know how good you've got it, kid. School was the best time of my life. A never-ending supply of wimps with candy. Those were the days. I'm surprised you haven't blown that place up yet, bad as you usually mess things up."

And on that cheery note, Duckwad pushed off with a splash because he wasn't a quiet kind of river troll.

"Me too," I answered under my breath. "Me too."

I didn't get to dwell on how I'd managed to attend the Three-Berry Academy for who knows how many years without losing my mind. My other uncle came paddling along before I could start wondering how I'd missed a chance to make a mistake that big. This uncle's name was Stump, and he often showed up right after his brother Duckwad passed through. Stump seemed to feel responsible for whatever damage his hatchmate had caused and always tried to repair the wreckage, first by slipping me a candied minnow or two.

"Don't mind him," Stump advised. "He's just all knotted up over some riddle that got dropped on him.

See? He never was good at those things and so takes it out on everyone else. That's all. That's his trouble, not yours. Say, you're not out here twisting around about school, are you? That's not what's up your snout, I hope, 'cause you know that none of us Fishflies have ever been so hot at that school stuff. Well maybe I-know was pretty good at it, but he probably don't count 'cause of that book he accidentally swallowed when he was younger."

"It's just that I make so many mistakes," I muttered.

"Oh it'd be a mistake to worry about that," Stump confided. "You inherited that fretfulness from your grandfather Who-do, and look how successful he's been. There's hardly anything he touches that doesn't start out a mistake and then turn into gold."

"Are you sure about that?"

"All night long," Stump assured me. "Want to know why?"

"Will it take long to tell me?" I waffled, thinking it might be a mistake to find out. My uncle Stump's stories usually raised more questions than they answered.

"Hasn't your mother ever told you about the magic clam that Who-do bought when he was a young troll? He probably wasn't much older than you are today. See?"

"She has," I sighed, hoping I wouldn't have to hear

that story again. Anybody with a pair of ears has heard about Grandfather's magic clam. It could talk.

"Good, 'cause it was the biggest mistake he ever made. The best one too. Just ask him sometime. He'll say. You know how he loves to talk."

"Boy do I." And he especially loved to talk with that magic clam of his. They argued everywhere they went, nonstop.

"Did you ever hear what that clam shouted at the king?" my uncle Stump asked, sunny as could be.

Oh dear. It was my grandfather's favorite clam story, but something told me it'd be a mistake to point that out.

"The king's a snail!" Uncle Stump half shouted. "That's what that clam shouted. Can you believe it?"

I could. That clam yelled something rude almost every day. But calling the king a snail—that was above and beyond his usual insults.

See, his royal highness, King Downsnout, had been feuding with the snails hereabouts for so long that nobody can exactly remember what started it, except that it had something to do with a snail, an open window, and the king's undies.

"Your grandfather nearly lost his head over that one," Uncle Stump chuckled. "Do you want to know why he didn't?"

"I'm not sure. Do I?" Now that I thought about it,

I'd never heard that part of the story explained.

"He talked his way out of it."

"I guess that makes sense," I reasoned. My grandfather gabbed pretty much nonstop.

"No it doesn't," Stump corrected. "Everyone says that when he was your age he was completely tongue-tied. Couldn't talk his way through saying hello without turning all purplish around the gills and hacky in the throat, 'cause he was terrified he'd say something wrong that would get him into trouble."

"Are you sure about that?"

"Sure as mud. Your great-grandmother loved to tell us all about it. She'd pinch our tongues with her claws and tell us to say something intelligent." Stump demonstrated by grabbing hold of his own tongue. "E oun-e ak i." Letting go of his tongue, he translated, "We sounded like that. And so did your Grandfather. Go on, try it."

"That's OK," I said. "I believe you. So how did grandfather ever manage to tell the king it was a clam who'd insulted him?"

"Because he didn't have anything to lose, that's how. See?"

"Anything but his head?" I ventured.

"That's right! And that's what untied his tongue. Yup. It took some explaining, you bet. And yet if he hadn't made the mistake of hauling that clam past the king's place, he might have never become the talker he is today. He wouldn't be talking anyone into doing anything. See?"

"I guess so." I frowned.

Turning it over in my mind, I had to admit that the story explained some things I'd never understood about my grandfather. For one thing, it explained why he dragged that clam with him everywhere he went.

At the same time, experience had taught me it was a huge mistake to listen too carefully to my uncle Stump's stories.

Why?

Because sooner or later Uncle Duckwad always doubled back to find out what was keeping him. Waiting around for that to happen was almost always a mistake, so I slipped away just as Stump moved on to remembering what the clam had once said to the biggest sturgeon on the river, which was another favorite tale and hardly worth going into at the moment, except to say that I'd sure never talk to a sturgeon that way.

My uncle's voice faded as I paddled around a bend. As mad as I was at myself for making the mistake of wasting time on one of his stories, I almost didn't hear the shout.

"Help!"

I mean, I heard it, but upset as I was about the

mistake of listening to my uncle, the word didn't register. Hard as I was swimming to get away from Stump, I wasn't paying attention to anyone but myself, which is another mistake that I don't ever seem to get tired of making. Good thing that whoever was in trouble had enough strength to call out again, louder.

"I said, HELP!"

That time the word registered, and I tore myself away from my mistakes long enough to double back to a sandbar I'd swum past. There was a clam stranded back there, beached two or three feet out of the water and sounding awfully put out about it

Of course by then it had dawned on me that I was dealing with a talking clam, which seemed kind of suspicious, rare as they are and what with my uncle Stump having just gone on and on about one. But thinking it might be a mistake to worry too much about coincidences when someone was yelling for help, I said instead, "What's the problem?"

"What do you think?" the clam answered, sounding as if I was a moron.

"How would I know? I just got here."

"Am I going to have to spell it out for you?" the clam asked.

By then I'd had plenty of time to wonder what kind of mistake I was about to make.

Big?

Or little?

It didn't take any genius to figure out that a mistake was headed my way and pretty fast. The tingling behind my ears was a dead giveaway. But as usual, I couldn't see any farther into the future than an earthworm who's just been introduced to a real friendly robin.

"I guess so," I answered, feeling pretty dumb. How many times have I been told that was a mistake? Feeling dumb, I mean.

"I am a clam," he said, speaking real slowly so that I wouldn't miss anything. "Are you with me so far?"

"I am."

"Good. Clams live in the water. Keeping up?"

"I think so."

"If I stay where I am, up here on this beach, sooner or later the sun's going to fry me. Make sense?"

"It does."

"SO THROW ME BACK INTO THE RIVER!"

It sure seemed like a mistake not to. But that tingling behind my ears? It kept getting worse. And that clam's voice . . . rude as it was, I was beginning to think that I'd heard it somewhere before.

"WHAT?" the clam yelled when I didn't budge. "Are you afraid of clams?"

"No," I answered, thinking that maybe it was a mistake not to be.

"So what's the holdup?"

I don't know how many times I've been asked that question. It pops up a lot, usually while I'm ticking off the best way to dodge all the mistakes that are whizzing my way faster than motorboats speeding down the river at night. Spotlights aimed my way freeze me every time.

"For crying out loud!" the clam screamed. "Just do it!"

And do you know what? I did, mostly because I can't stand being screamed at, which was probably another mistake.

But by then I was fed up with all the mistakes that had been piling up around me since I'd rolled out of my nest that night. I didn't care if I made one more. What difference could it make? So I grabbed that clam, cocked my arm, and reared back. Oh yeah. I planned to throw that clam so far out into the channel that I'd never have to hear his miserable voice again.

Boy was that a mistake.

There was a noose buried in the sand beneath that clam. A noose that wrapped itself around me the instant I touched the clam's shell. Into the air the noose whipped me. When my vision cleared, I found myself dangling upside down from a towering cottonwood. My arms were pinned against my side by rope, and the clam was gripped in my paw.

"Now what?" groused the clam.

I would have started making excuses, even if it is nearly always a mistake, but my Grandfather Who-do showed up before I could get started. Uncle Stump and Uncle Duckwad were right behind him. The three of them stood beneath me and that clam, watching us sway back and forth as if we were the best show they'd seen in weeks.

"Iffy," my grandfather congratulated, "looks like you're in the middle of some kind of mistake."

"A whopper," Uncle Stump tsked.

"I told him," Uncle Duckwad added.

"So?" I said.

"Do you want to know what's the biggest mistake a river troll can make?" Grandfather asked.

"I don't know, do I?"

"It'd be a mistake not to," said Stump.

"You little pipsqueak," Duckwad added.

"All right," I said, "tell me."

"Being afraid to make a mistake," Grandfather answered. "That's the biggest one. That's why I'm loaning you my clam."

"What good's that going to do?" I asked.

"It'll help teach you how big mistakes can get," Grandfather answered.

"Is that really necessary?"

"Once you see the size of the mistakes that clam

can make, you'll quit worrying about your little mess-ups. Believe me."

"It's for your own good," Uncle Stump helpfully explained.

"Next time you better have more minnows," Duckwad warned.

And without another word my grandfather and two uncles dove into the river and swam off, leaving me with a clam who had called the king a snail.

"Now what?" the clam demanded to know.

"School," I told him, figuring that things couldn't get much worse. Talk about wrong.

"Good," the clam said. "I'll get your teacher straightened out in nothing flat."

What had all my years at the Three-Berry taught me about Quiet Quickthorn? That this clam was about to make the biggest mistake of his life. Wrong again.

"Maybe we should invite the king," the clam went on. "The fool might learn a thing or two about snails."

When I heard that I broke down laughing. I couldn't help it. It was either that or cry. I was already looking fondly back at the little mistakes I'd been worrying about just that morning.

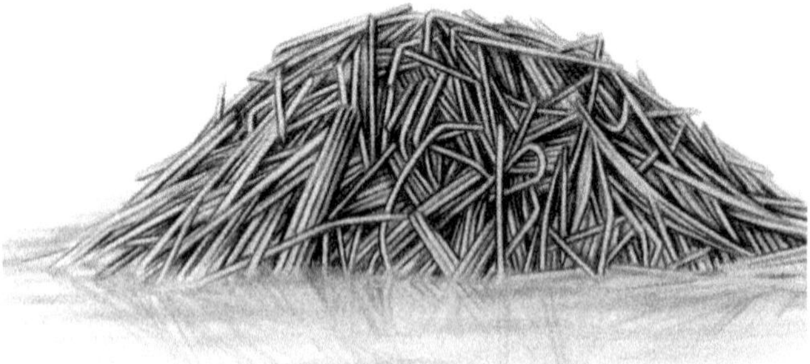

Precocious Grabsome

"How old are you anyway?"

"Twenty-six."

"I've my doubts about that. And even if you are, it's still too young to be going to school."

"I'll give you my best turtle shell."

"What else?"

"A promise."

"What kind?"

"To get straight A's."

"I don't like the sound of that. They'll know you're

not me in a flash."

"Not if I tell them you're under a spell."

"Got an answer for everything, don't you? What's your big hurry to get to school anyway?"

"I just don't want to wait. That's all. It sounds like too much fun."

"Fun! Have you ever woke up with a crawdad pinching your snout?"

"Sure, but—"

"Ever have a dream where the whole river ran through your ears?"

"Not exactly, but—"

"How about sharing your last minnow? Ever had to do that?"

"I don't see what—"

"'Cause that's how much fun going to the good old Three-Berry Academy is. And don't try to tell me you know different, not till you've sat in one of those desks for a night."

"If it's so bad, maybe you should pay me to take your place."

"Nice try. But I don't think so. Now, you mentioned your best turtle shell, what else you got to sweeten the pot? And don't go bothering with any more promises. I might call the whole deal off if you bring up those A's again."

"How about an anchor rope?"

"Maybe. Got the anchor?"

"'Fraid not."

"Then forget it."

"Wait a minute. I've got a catfish whisker."

The smaller troll held the whisker up for inspection. It looked fairly new, hardly used at all. Still had some twitch to it.

"Where'd you get it?"

"Does it matter?"

"Maybe not. All right, hand it over."

"Not until you show me where your baited snare is."

"Don't trust me, huh?"

"Not at all."

"Kid, you just might pull this off. But I got to warn you about one thing. When Burpetta Sludgeton starts picking on you, you're going to be all on your own."

"No problem."

"I wouldn't be so sure about that."

"I would. Tutu Mudnose owes me a big favor, and I think he can handle Burpetta."

"Geez. You've got all the angles covered, don't you? I give up. Follow me. She puts my bait on that rock over there."

"What kind of bait?"

"Doesn't much matter. She knows I can't resist marshmallows, and she always smothers whatever it is with them. You give me the marshmallows and it's a deal. I'll let you take my place. I've seen enough of the Three-Berry to last me till this river starts blowing bubbles. If I have to spend one more year watching Two Shellcruncher wave her paw all over the place because she thinks she knows some answer, I might turn into an eel.

"Come over here. Just check out that rock. Soon as you scoop up the marshmallows, a snare's going to nab your tail and jerk you up to that branch way up there."

"You're sure?"

"Happened every year so far. Twenty or fifty times at least, I've been hanging in the breeze up there, waiting to be picked up for school. I don't think I'm going to miss—hey! Where's my marshmallows?"

They stood side-by-side, facing a bare rock.

"I don't see anything."

"If she thinks she can catch me without any bait . . ."

In their haste, they both stepped onto the rock to check if the marshmallows had tumbled off the back side, and sure enough, they had. Neither of them had a chance to reach for them though.

The instant they touched the rock, a snare closed around both their tails at once and up they flew.

"What's next?" the younger troll asked, thrilled.

"Roll call," the older troll answered, defeated.
"What's that? I love it already."

Wabash Smoothwater

"ALL I WANT TO DO IS HAVE FUN!!!"

That was me, Wabash Smoothwater, addressing the entire world after the last night of school the previous spring. At that moment summer vacation stretched out before me, wider and more shimmering than the river at sunset.

"What's fun?" my mother wanted to know.

But even a question as wrong as that failed to slow me down.

"I can tell you what it's not," I whooped. "It's

not sniffing thick old books that Quiet Quickthorn is thumping on her desk. If I never catch another whiff of *The History of Important Trolls* or *How Rivers Work* or *The Theory of Counting*, it will be too soon."

"Fair enough," my mother agreed, for she wasn't much of a sniffer of books herself.

"And," I stormed on, "fun is not listening to Two Shellcruncher blabber on every time the teacher tries to stump the class with a question."

"Well I can guarantee that you won't be anywhere near a Shellcruncher this summer," Mother promised. She refused to have anything to do with that entire clan ever since the days she'd been a student herself.

"And," I continued after a deep breath, "fun especially has nothing to do with old Quiet Quickthorn herself. She could suck the fun out of a juicy clam without even opening her mouth."

"Glad to hear it," Mother said. "That means I won't have to try to get on her good side by inviting her over for slough tea and crunch. Anything else?"

"No. Just so long as I have FUN."

"Fun?" Mother repeated. "I'll get right on that. Tomorrow evening, dusky and early, you'll be having loads of fun up on this lodge's roof."

"What's fun up there?"

"For starters, the chimney. We're going to repack the mud around it."

I wrinkled my snout.

"Don't give me that look," Mother warned. "It will be a blast. So long as you stay clear of the wasps. And after that we're going to re-thatch the roof. You can't imagine what a riot that will be. And then I'm thinking we need to dig out the pantry. There's been a lot of silt settling in back there. We'll have the time of our lives with it."

I pinched the tip of my snout as if catching a nasty whiff of something sweet and terrible. "Anything else?"

"Don't you worry," Mother comforted. "I'm sure there's plenty more fun where that came from. I want you to have the time of your life this summer. Speaking of which, I'd say it's past time for you to turn in."

"But it's still dark out," I protested, not at all ready for bed, not on the first night of summer vacation.

"If you're going to have fun, you want to start out all rested up, don't you? Go on now, off you go. And no whispering with your sisters."

I went, mumbling. My sisters followed, stepping on my tail and blaming me for the early bedtime but knowing better than to try talking their way into staying up late. Our mother wasn't the sort of troll who changed her mind for anything less than a flash flood, and sometimes not even for that.

But it turned out that Mother could see farther

into the future than we gave her credit for. She was absolutely right about our needing every bit of rest we could get.

The next night the sun had barely set than we were filling our dugout canoe with mud from the neighborhood bottoms and hauling it up onto our roof, where we pried loose the cracked, dried stuff that was barely holding our chimney together.

Several ungrateful wasp families woke up to give us a hand.

Not that being stung by a wasp hurt a thick-skinned river troll, but it was supposed to be bad luck. And sure enough, I got stung five times and it took five nights of backbreaking work to finish repacking the chimney.

Or at least I thought it took that long. With numbers that high, who can be sure? And that was only the start of the summer's fun.

Mother quickly moved us on to collecting new thatch for our roof. Cutting and piling reeds was almost as good a time as hauling mud. And we didn't even get a night off to rest our blisters.

It was weeks after school ended before we got any time off, and then only because we'd reached mid-June, or the Midsummer Ooze, as we call it along the river. Any troll with half a tail knew that you didn't go bumbling around on the shortest night of the year, not without getting into trouble.

Or at least that's what my mother claimed. That was just asking for a punch in the snout, she said. All the scariest stories, the ones that had sent me and my hatchmates diving under the covers when we were small, all took place on that night.

But this year I saw it as my big chance to find out if maybe Mother wasn't covering something up, for I'd begun to think that all the grownups I knew complained a little too much about the Midsummer Ooze. It seemed suspicious.

"Outlandish," my Aunt Chipped-tooth would always declare with a wink at my mother.

"Totally uncalled for," my Uncle Too-sweet agreed after a cough.

"Over my dead body," my mother told us whenever we risked asking if maybe this year we weren't old enough to go see what all the Ooze fuss was about.

Of course me and my hatchmates had heard stories at school about what happened on that night, particularly over to the Yellow Cat Bottoms. Our classmates claimed that blue-wing fairies danced and sang over there until the first light of day drove them off.

What's more, they said you could tell which trolls had been there because they couldn't stop grinning for weeks afterwards, not even in a hail storm. And for months afterwards they might giggle or titter or hee-haw at the strangest times, like say when passing the clam sauce at dinner.

If they were having that much fun over there, I wanted my share, especially after spending an entire year chained to a school desk at the Three-Berry Academy with old Quiet Quickthorn breathing down my neck. Well, all right, maybe I hadn't been exactly chained there, but it sure felt that way. You try sitting in front of Two Shellcruncher and see.

So as soon as possible that night, I excused myself from the game of snap-shell in the living room and slipped out my bedroom window, letting the current carry me away without so much as a ripple. I didn't leave a note either. What was the fun in that?

Along I drifted, floating over the old convertible car that had been parked on the bottom of Big Mouth Slough for years. The seat-belted skeleton behind the steering wheel had been grinning the whole time.

I slid past turtles who had backed into the tall grasses and pulled in their heads as soon as the sun had set.

Once I reached the main channel I figured it was safe to start swimming upstream to the Yellow Cat Bottoms. No one back home would be able to hear me splash from that far away.

An hour later I was wading through bull rushes and pondweed toward a light that was bright enough to cast shadows. Normally the slightest hint of a shadow was enough to make me cut and run, but tonight all the laughter I heard, along with a tinkling sound that floated on the air, pulled me forward.

Twice I had to duck when blue-wing fairies spiraled by overhead, flying toward the light.

Tea-cup sized, the fairies' glowing wings and handsome faces, which shone like small moons, dropped my jaw every time. The way their wings hummed was a song all in itself, and when one of them spotted me, she hovered long enough to say, "Don't be shy. All are welcome."

She flitted off, leaving me with the notion that I'd just woken from the worst smelling dream I'd ever had. Dreams don't get any better than that.

Touching my snout, I discovered I was grinning!

From then on I didn't waste any time but crashed across the marsh until reaching the light, where I skidded to a stop.

A huge bonfire burned atop the water, showing the faces of the creatures gathered around it.

Bearded giants beat on log drums with wooden spoons big enough to stir laundry.

Elves ran and slid across the water as if it was frozen.

A handful of wizards stood waist deep in the water, beaming at the blaze as if they'd just invented fire.

Dwarves in lifejackets were crowded into boats, their heads bobbing up and down in time to the music, which seemed to come from the flames and sounded elfin, bringing to mind high clouds under a silvery moon.

But most amazing of all were the dozens of fairies crisscrossing over the bonfire. Their glowing wings reflected the reds and greens and purples of the flames, speckling the entire marsh with color that never stopped dancing.

When a golden fish raised her head out of the water and asked me to, "Join us," she didn't have to ask twice.

I found myself making faces at an elf . . . swatting my tail against a log drum . . . harmonizing with a pontoon-load of dwarves . . . trying to count . . . trying to fly . . . reaching toward the stars while floating on my back . . . tingling . . . pinching myself . . . plucking a harp as if I'd been playing one all my life . . . Rubbing snouts with a—well, I wasn't sure what it was . . . and wishing that the night would never end.

I felt that way right up to the moment that I found myself snout-to-snout with another river troll.

My first thought was to turn away, pretend I hadn't bumped into anyone, and flee into the night before this troll recognized me. The last thing I needed was for my mother to hear on the grapevine that I'd sneaked off to the Ooze. That'd be the start of a whole new round of fun at home, and I didn't think I could stand any more of that.

But just as I was about to slip away, the troll's nearest orange eye winked at me.

It was a slow, heavy-lidded wink that seemed to take an hour or more to hit bottom. And when this troll's eyelid did finally close entirely shut it crashed so loudly that I lurched as if something made of glass, something priceless and irreplaceable, had just been smashed to smithereens.

It was at that exact moment that I realized I knew the troll facing me.

Worse, I also figured out that the troll knew me as well.

You see, the troll's other eye, the one remaining open, was roving all over the place, taking in the heavens and the bottoms and the drumming giants and spinning blue wings and everything. So far as I knew, there was only one troll with an eye that could do all that, and it belonged to Quiet Quickthorn.

The crash that had made me flinch? It must have been the sound of me imagining my teacher shattering into a thousand tiny pieces.

Worse, Quiet Quickthorn was grinning like a rock troll baking popovers.

That just seemed wrong.

The possibility that my teacher could ever enjoy anything other than making students squirm turned my brain into a block of ice. Whatever I thought of saying skidded away before it could slip out my mouth.

And then Quiet Quickthorn held a claw up to her lips as if to say *Let's keep this our little secret, shall we?* And without another word, she paddled off toward a canoe full of dwarves who were calling to her like old friends.

I stayed behind, trying to piece my world back together.

How long I stood there falling apart is hard to say. It felt longer than clocks or calendars or history books could measure.

All that came to an abrupt end when a sudden flurry of sparks swirled upward from the bonfire, drawing everyone's attention.

After the last of the sparks had flared and died against the brightening sky, those gathered pivoted slowly to the east where spokes of scarlet sunlight were streaming over the Wisconsin bluffs.

In a thrice everyone was skittering, flickering, diving, striding for cover as the bonfire vanished instantly, without a trace of smoke left behind. There wasn't so much as a dimple dotting the water where it'd been.

At the same instant the sound of one last plucked harp string faded into the wooded bluffs all around me.

I scanned everywhere without catching so much as a glimpse of my teacher.

Finding myself alone, I too hurried off with an unfinished sentence trapped inside my head. "That couldn't have been . . ."

That unfinished sentence haunted me for the rest of the summer. It made everything I did seem slightly out of focus and not quite real.

At night my dreams were filled with grinning snouts and winking eyes. Even my mother's idea of fun failed to make me grumble as the question hummed inside my head night and day.

That couldn't have been . . . That couldn't have been . . . That couldn't have been . . . That couldn't have been . . .

Finally I decided the only way to get any peace was to find out if it really was Quiet Quickthorn I'd seen at the Midsummer Ooze. But how?

I wasn't brave enough to go to the Quickthorn lodge alone. All that left me with was returning to school in the fall, and even then I wasn't exactly sure what I could do.

Asking my teacher directly seemed out of the question, especially after the troll I'd met had put a claw to her lips to signal we should keep everything our little secret.

Maybe there'd be other clues I could detect. Duckweed stuck between my teacher's teeth, or an unexpected grin when nothing was funny.

Or I could try mentioning the Yellow Cat Bottoms and see if my teacher blinked.

Or I could raise my hand and ask if the academy had any books about the Midsummer Ooze.

Or if none of that worked, perhaps I could summon the courage to try winking at my teacher.

I'd just have to pay close attention and see what would happen. And plotting all that turned out to be the most fun I had all summer. When the time came, I stepped into the first snare I happened across. Never paid a bit of attention to its bait.

Booky Doublemuck

Students at the Three-Berry Academy for the Totally Gifted can graduate by either finishing the top grade or sticking around until they're a hundred.

Of course nobody's trusted to keep track of their age themselves. Poor as us trolls count and much as most of us want summer vacation to never end, half of Three-Berry's students would claim they were a hundred every year.

No, the only way anyone knows they've reached a hundred is when that old lady over in Big Rock gives us a birthday cake.

You know the old lady I mean? The one who runs that rivery store with all the troll junk in it.

She also keeps track of our ages for a fee and hands out the puniest cakes you can imagine. They amount to half a bite, if that much, but that cake's what marks the end of most students' education.

I said *most*.

And then there's me, Booky Doublemuck. Last spring that old bag in Big Rock said I'd hit a hundred and Quiet Quickthorn graduated me—AGAINST MY WISHES!

I spent the entire summer trying to come up with some way to get back into the Three- Berry. Why? Because there isn't anywhere I love more than school.

Rumor has it that I'd petitioned the school for re-admission as a first grader and been turned down. Well let me tell you—that ain't no rumor!

I offered to take someone else's seat, but troll parents along the river were up in arms about that one. They didn't want their kids home, any more than the kids wanted to be there.

All right, I tried threatening to die of heartache and come back as a ghost. Quiet Quickthorn squelched that one by pointing out I'd already graduated, which mean I couldn't come back as a ghost.

So I was desperate.

That's why I was swimming downstream in search of the wishing orchard. Legend had it that anyone brave enough to gobble down an apple from that place was granted a wish.

I had no idea what an apple tasted like but expected the worst. Humans ate them, didn't they? That didn't slow me down though. I was willing to gobble up a whole basket of the things if it meant I could make a wish to stay in school. But first I had to find Lipsome Slice-toe, who screened all trolls to make sure their wishes were worthy of the orchard.

"Who's waking me up now?" Lipsome crabbed when I stopped outside his lodge and burped, which is the polite way for a river troll to announce his or her presence.

At the moment I was treading water in front of the strangest lodge I had ever seen. It was the back-end of an old wagon whose front end (and maybe the horse that pulled it) was buried in the riverbank below the waterline.

A saggy lawn chair that must have fallen off a passing boat was set up beneath the wagon. Lipsome was slumped in that chair. He'd pulled a tarp up to his chin, which had a bumper crop of Spanish moss hanging off it. Minnows darted in and out of the moss.

Even Lipsome didn't know how old he was, though he claimed to have hatched below a castle that was crumbling slowly into the river where he learned to swim. The name of that river escaped him, but he was pretty sure it wasn't the Mississippi.

One of his eyes was sealed shut by a leech. All his freckles had blossomed into warts so long ago that time had worn them back down into freckles.

His teeth were too white for homegrown and sharper than everything but his tongue.

"Don't answer that," Lipsome snapped before I could identify myself. "I suppose you're here for the orchard, but just what makes you think there is one?"

"I sniffed it in a book."

"Oh you did, did you? And do you believe everything your nose tells you?"

"Depends on how it smells."

"Don't think I haven't heard that line before. I've heard every kind of nonsense to be found. The question is, will I believe you? First off, you better tell me about your clan. That will give me some idea."

So I recited my foremothers and –fathers, going so far back that Lipsome dozed off at one point.

When the old gatekeeper woke up and discovered I was still naming relatives, he grumbled, "Enough! I get the idea. You're a grand and illustrious bunch. Invented water and give eel-grass to the poor. All well and good, though I do want to clarify one minor point. I knew your great-great-great grandfather Glorious Doublemuck, and I wouldn't have trusted him to carry mud. But at least you didn't try to pretend he belonged to some other clan of Doublemucks. You claimed him. Fair enough. So here's the deal. I can't let just anybody go wandering up to that orchard and making a wish. Do you have any idea what would happen if I did?"

"I'm afraid not."

"Let me spell it out for you then. Last year I had a Logrot out here who wanted to turn every troll in the valley into a butterfly. She was growing horns and spitting fire because she hadn't been invited to the spring-flood royal feast. She was going to teach everyone a lesson for slighting her. So what do you think would have happened if I'd let her go tearing up to the orchard with a wish like that?"

"Right now we'd be sitting on flowers?"

Lipsome sized me up with his one good eye and spat off to the side, which is never a pretty sight when you're underwater.

"That's about right," the gatekeeper agreed. "And I hate flowers. They make my warts itch. So I suggested to her, in as kind and thoughtful a voice as I could muster—" here the old troll was nearly shouting "—that she should aim her sights a little lower and think—JUST MAYBE—about wishing for an invitation to the feast instead of turning everyone into butterflies. What do you think of that?"

"Sounds reasonable," I allowed.

"Goes to show how much you know about that orchard. Reasonable doesn't have anything to do with what goes on up there. But she agreed to it, and so I let her by, though she couldn't let well enough alone. Logrots rarely can. So what's she do when she gets up there? Wishes for an invitation to the head of the table, she does."

And there Lipsome Slice-toe stopped.

I tilted forward, wanting to hear the rest, but the gatekeeper eased back in his lawn chair as if he enjoyed seeing me on hooks and anchors. The old troll batted a perch away from his leech-covered eye.

He grinned.

A creaking sound accompanied the grin.

He briefly verged on nodding off.

Finally I couldn't take the suspense any longer and blurted out what the old troll wanted to hear.

"What happened then?"

"She got her wish. The orchard turned her into a gigantic smoked sturgeon on a platter that was placed at the head of the banquet table. The last anyone saw of that Logrot, she was headed toward the King's mouth. Questions?"

"Is that true?"

"Do I look like I've got time to sit around making

things up?"

Actually that's exactly what Lipsome Slice-toe looked like he had time to do, but I had spent so many years reading Quiet Quickthorn's moods when she asked the class a question that I knew better than to say yes. "No, sir."

"That's putting it mildly," Lipsome grumbled. "Is that true? Why, I've half a mind—" But then the gatekeeper dropped it, muttering, "At least you're paying attention. So why do you think I told you all that? DON'T ANSWER THAT!!!! You'll straighten out my tail all over again. I told you so that you'd take this wishing business seriously. This orchard's nothing to fool around with. Some of the stuff I've seen it do could put hair on a clam. So tell me—what's so important that you had to come all the way out here for a wish?"

"Well, sir, I ah . . ."

"And make it snappy! I don't have all night."

"I don't want to quit school," I blurted.

"So don't. Who's stopping you? Got a mother who thinks she knows better?"

"No, sir. Well, yes, sir. But she's not the reason—"

"Well, what then? I've had a barge load of whippersnappers out here wishing they could quit school, but you're the first one who wanted to stay in it. I smell something fishy, and I don't mean the good kind of fishy either. What gives?"

"I turned one hundred this summer," I confessed.

"I hit four hundred and something myself. Tell me something important."

"The school I go to won't let you stay past a hundred."

"Sensible."

"But I don't want to leave. I really like it there, learning things."

"That's all?" Lipsome dug a claw around in his ear as if maybe he'd missed something. "You know you're only going to get one trip out to this orchard, don't you? In your whole life, I mean."

"I've heard that."

"And that's what you want to waste it on? Most come up with something more river worthy than that kind of piffle. A handsome tail or brand-new lodge or squirming out of some crushing debt or falling in love . . . but more school? That takes the clam. Well, all right. I guess you can't get into too much trouble with that one. You're sure your mind's made up?"

"I am. School's where I'm happiest."

"If you say so."

And without another word, Lipsome pushed open the gate barring the mouth of the creek that led to the wishing orchard. Built of flood junk—bicycles and ripped screen doors and orange road cones—the gate was heavy and hard to push. I had to lend a paw and even then we almost couldn't budge it.

The last thing Lipsome said as he waved me through wasn't what you'd call comforting. "You need to be outside more. Build yourself up."

I didn't answer. Swimming upstream against the creek's current sapped all my strength. I kept at it though, clinging to a root or boulder whenever I needed to rest.

The creek's water was pure glass compared to the river's murkiness, and I spied the stars above as if there wasn't any water protecting me at all.

That was a pinch scary, like being on dry land, so I quit looking up.

Different kinds of fish flashed by. I saw my first rainbow trout gleaming like heated metal, but I forged ahead without another look because I was racing against the dawn. Once the sun flattened out the world, I didn't want to be anywhere but underwater if I could help it.

At one point I heard splashing, followed by slurping, and I pulled up short to watch a four-legged creature with a bell around its neck drinking from the creek. I shied past it, not liking how large her eyes were. The Three-Berry taught that big eyes meant big teeth meant trouble.

I passed other eyes too. Eyes that glinted out of

underwater burrows or peeked down from overhanging branches, and they spurred me forward faster and faster.

Though the creek grew narrower, at least it stayed deep enough to keep me covered, but as long as that creek was, I needed most of the night to reach the small pond at its end. The stars above were pulling down their shades against the morning light just as I got there.

Into the pond I plunged, staying submerged as I searched for the wishing orchard. By the time I figured out that there weren't any apple trees under the water, the night was all used up.

Desperate, I surfaced, only to be greeted by the thin gray light that melts away quickly as daylight crashes over the world.

Spinning about, I realized that the entire pond was surrounded by trees.

I couldn't be sure if they were apple trees because I'd never seen one before, but I thought there was a good chance they were. They smelled like the book that held pictures of the wishing orchard, and where else would I find them? The pond only had one way in and out and that was the creek I'd followed.

I was trying to talk myself into swimming over to the closest tree when one last piece of night broke loose from a shadow and flew straight toward me. I was about to dive straight to the bottom of the pond when I saw that whatever was moving toward me had wings and black feathers, except on its head, which was bald. I thought it might be a crow, which would explain the cawing but not the fact that it could talk. Circling above me, it delivered a message.

"One wish. One wish."

The bird flapped away just as the first rays of sunlight ignited the trees surrounding me.

Everywhere I turned, golden fruit flashed and beckoned. I had to shield my eyes, but then I figured out that ducking a foot or two underwater made it possible to look without being blinded.

Swimming to the nearest tree, I discovered a branch that I could reach and plucked the lowest hanging apple on it. The thing was roughly the size of a turtle egg, though not as perfectly round. Its golden skin reflected my snout.

Holding the fruit in front of myself, I could take in my entire face's reflection in the apple's curved surface. It made my head seem huge, which somehow gave me the courage to do what needed to be done. Down the hatch went the apple. In two bites it was gone and I made my wish.

I never want to leave school

The apple halves tumbled down my throat like boulders, scraping all the way.

For a second I thought that I might choke or gag, coughing them back up. But fearing that would be the end of my wish, I kept them down, and they soon landed in my first stomach. The splash they made sounded strangely like a bell whose ringing was spreading through my entire body.

And that was when I understood that I'd been all wrong about what the orchard would do.

I had assumed it would change the Three-Berry's rules so that I wouldn't have to leave just because I'd graduated. Or maybe my wish would just make me young so that I could start school all over.

But that was how a troll thought, not a wishing orchard. To a magical orchard, the simplest thing to do was turn me into something that would never leave the school, something like a bell, one that could fit in the tower above the academy.

Looking down, I discovered that I wasn't surrounded by the orchard anymore.

Furthermore, that where I'd once had a body of scales, I now had a silver bell.

Where I'd once had a tail, I now had a clapper. Tied to the end of the clapper was the snare that Quiet Quickthorn had been using for years to catch me. Spread out below the end of the rope was the Three-Berry Academy's classroom, perfect as ever.

A passing catfish tugged on the rope, making me

clang with a pure silvery note that left me happier than I'd ever thought possible. I was back in school for good.

Collection Day

By the time I sent the Three-Berry Academy's collection raft after my students, most of them had been hanging upside-down for at least a night and were almost starting to look forward to classes.

A sniffle could be heard here and there, but that dried up the instant they saw who was coming for them. Their rescuers were some rocks trolls who looked friendly as flaming brick houses falling out of a stormy sky.

Instead of scales they had flaky quartz for skin.

No willow hair, just crinkly crystals.

Their eyes were bulgier than a river troll's. Their snouts snoutier.

They had dents here and there where you'd least expect them.

One look at them left you wondering if something heavy had flattened them, or if they had fallen off a cliff, or what.

Why did I use rock trolls to round up my students? Mostly because river trolls were too likely to go soft and let my catches go.

Rock trolls, they hardly know the meaning of pity. Their hearts are nothing but crushed gravel in a bag.

Also, the rock trolls I used were sons of Contrary Rockslide. I'd once saved her from drowning, so they worked for free, which was good. I couldn't see paying for their help 'cause they weren't the sharpest slabs underground.

Matter of fact, I had to swim after the raft to make sure they didn't do something brilliant, like untie my students so they could push the raft. I once lost a whole class that way.

From largest to smallest, the Rockside brothers were named Vroom, who was so afraid of brooms that he couldn't pronounce it right.

Then came Tomtom, who thought he was supposed to be twins.

And last came Savious, who spent most of his

time saving his brothers from doing something their mother wouldn't like.

Vroom had the highest reach of the three and used a saw tied to the end of a TV antenna to cut my students down from their snares.

Tomtom caught each one, tied them up with the snare that had snagged them, and stacked them at the center of the raft like so much firewood.

Savious stood at the back of the raft, holding several oars that were lashed together. He used them to pole on toward the next snare. Being the brains of the outfit, Savious also read the map that showed each snare's whereabouts.

All of the brothers had a wobbly, nervous look about them, as if they just knew the raft was going to tip over any moment. Boulderish and awkward as they were, it was a real possibility. And none of them were wearing life vests because they couldn't find any that were huge enough.

The possibility of falling into the river made them kind of sparky. Being rock trolls, the only thing they knew how to do in water was sink.

"Just asks her," Savious crabbed at his brothers, who at the moment were trying to peek in the ear of the last student they'd collected.

"Aint's it better to just looks and sees?" Tomtom asked.

"You can't sees anything inside a river troll's head," Savious scoffed.

"Ain'ts nothing but clamshells and sand rattling around in there," Vroom added, puffing up as if he was some kind of brain surgeon.

"But what if she lies?" Tomtom complained.

"Of course she'll lies. She's a river troll, ain'ts she?"

"Well, yes."

"And we're rock trolls, ain'ts we?"

"Did someone say we weren't?" Vroom demanded.

"So she'll lies," Savious went on.

"Then what's the point of asking?" Tomtom said.

"To gets her thinking, you knothead."

"Oh."

"So asks."

Leaning over, Tomtom poked the newest student's shoulder and crossly said, "Do you likes numbers?"

"What kinds of numbers?" the river troll squeaked in an I'm-about-to-wet-my-tail kind of way. She was on the small side and large as her eyes were open, she must have been a new student at the Three-Berry Academy.

Rock trolls don't get big by dieting, and once they are big, they spend a good deal of their time thinking about staying big by eating. And there were always stories—rumors, really—that their cookbooks had a section on how to prepare river trolls. It was usually said to be the part right before desserts.

"There's more than one kind of numbers?" Vroom asked, sounding shocked.

"Who cares?" Savious groused. "Just asks if she likes the kind that comes one right after another."

Tomtom did the honors.

"Why would numbers do that?" the young troll asked, shocked.

"This might be a good one to takes home," Vroom said, impressed by that question.

"Now *why* would we wants to do that?" Savious groaned.

"You knows how Mamakins always say we don't asks enough questions?" Vroom reasoned. "Well, thinks of all the questions this one could give us to asks."

"That wouldn't leads us anywhere but to the worst kinds of trouble," Savious stated.

"It wouldn'ts?" Although Vroom acted surprised, he didn't act totally surprised. The worst kinds of troubles didn't sound like any stranger to him.

"Did it ever occurs to you," Savious lectured, "that if we took one of these croakers home with us that one of the others would notice and tell their teacher? And who do you think she would tell?

"Mamakins?" Vroom winced.

"And what do you thinks she would do?"

"Takes away our crickets?"

"For starters."

"But what if we took the other one home with us too?" Tomtom suggested.

"Which other one, you pebble-brain?"

"The other one who's going to tells their teacher that we took the first one. Then Mamakins wouldn't finds out nothing."

"Why isn't that just brilliant?" Savious sneered, threatening to whack him with an oar, which probably explained why they were so splintered. "Don't you thinks that one of the ones left might notice if we took more than one of them?"

"I supposed," Tomtom conceded.

"And then what do you thinks might happen?"

"He might tell his teacher?" Vroom guessed.

"Maybe we could asks him real nice not to tells their teacher," Tomtom suggested.

"You can't trusts a croaker who's in a spot like that," Savious snorted.

"Waits a minute!" Vroom bugled. "I've gots it. We'll just take the one who's going to tell that we took the others. Then we'd be in the clear."

"Of all the—"

"Whats?" Vroom cried. "We can keeps him in that

back cavern we've been digging on. Mamakins never goes back there."

"And what about the next one who'd tells we tooks the others?" Savious asked, sounding impatient enough to explode.

"Wells," Vroom careful considered, "I guess we'd have to takes him too. But thats shouldn't be a problem. That new cavern's plenty big enough to . . ."

"Enough!" Savious shouted. "The point is that we'd have to takes all of them or nones of them because any we delivers to that school is going to tells what happened to the others."

"So then, all of them then," Vroom huffed, sounding put out. "Maybe we could stash some of them down to Gravelgut's place."

Savious stared up at the stars above them for a few heartbeats, muttering before finally asking, "And just what are we going to tell Quiet Quickthorn when we shows up with an empty raft?"

"How abouts we say that one of them giant squid things cames along and grabbed them all?" Tomtom generally got a monster from the deep worked into his excuses.

The idea certainly gave the Rockslide brothers something to think over.

And while I watched them doing that, the eyes of the youngest river trolls on the raft got big, and then bigger, at the thought of never being able to finish their education but ending up in the dark room of some dark cave that was probably filled with screeching rock birds and lying cave crickets and giant earthworms that wanted to cuddle.

The older students, the ones who'd been hearing the Rockslide brothers carry on this same argument for years, mostly looked steamed that they'd been caught yet again. It was one of them who finally ended the talk about giant squids by saying in a bored voice, "There aren't any giant squids around here."

"We don't knows that," Savious said.

"No. But our teacher does."

"Ah." Savious snapped his stony claws together, knowing that he'd been overlooking something. "That's whats I was forgetting. So it's all or nothing, boys, and I says nothing, because I don't wants to be the one who has to tell Mamakins we gots a cavern full of her friend's students. Does you?"

The two others couldn't agree fast enough with that. So onwards they rafted, collecting the last few students and pushing on toward my schoolhouse, where they had to ignore their watering mouths and unload students without tasting even so much as a lick's worth of them.

I took it from there, welcoming my students and telling them to float on the surface until everyone was off the raft.

"Please."

The iron way I snapped that one word, combined with the roving of my eyes, which covered almost everywhere at once, made sure that nobody dared disobey. Perhaps a few of the older students were biding their time, just waiting for a chance to make a break for it, but I sure couldn't tell by looking at them. For now they were all mine.

Once the raft was empty and my students were bobbing in the water, I lined them up in rows and asked if they had something to say to the Rockslide brothers for getting them all safely to school.

Straining not to glance at one another out of the corners of their orange eyes, the students sang out as one, "Thank you."

One first-year student, who didn't know any better, tacked on at the end, "For not eating us."

I spun around so fast that most of the students barely had time to snap their mouths shut.

Of course all I found was a field of innocent snouts, though if I'd had eyes in the back of my head, the way that graduates of the Three-Berry have always claimed I did, I'd have noticed that the Rockslide brothers looked slightly honored by that last bit, as though at least someone realized how dangerous they were.

"Very well," I slowly said, my vision sweeping across the students. "We'll work on that. And now I believe these brave rock trolls have a start-of-school present for each of you."

"We does?" Vroom miserably whispered.

"We does," Savious sighed. Raising his voice, he went on, "Students of The Three-Berry Academy for the Totally Gifted, we has gifts for you."

"Does we haves to?" Tomtom begged.

"You knows we does," Savious grunted. "If we wants any supper when we gets home."

That cinched it.

The Rockslide brothers arranged themselves more or less in a straight line and tried their best to put on brave faces.

Vroom looked as if a giant squid had just counted his toes.

Tomtom as if he'd just been asked to dance.

And Savious as if a cave cricket had called out his name.

"We'd likes to—" Savious started out but didn't get a chance to finish because he had to grab on to his brothers' arms to keep them from edging away. They acted ready to jump into the river rather than do what came next.

Once Savious had a hold of his brothers, he started all over again. "We'd like to give each of you a number that'll be yours to keep and take care of—"

"—And remember," I spliced in.

"And cherish," Savious agreed with a shudder, "for the rest of your lives."

The newest students silently gasped, speechless as leeches in a new boot, for suddenly they understood why these rock trolls had asked if they liked numbers.

They never got a chance to hide behind their tails though.

I started applauding Savious' announcement before anyone could whip out their tails. One of the older students had enough sense to follow my lead and start clapping too.

The others quickly joined in, which may have been what saved the night because for an instant there the Rockslide brothers had looked rattled enough to forget their mother's warnings and do a little rampaging, which is generally what a rock troll does best.

But when the students' applause washed over them, they settled down and took some sheepish bows.

Vroom bent over so far that he lost his balance, fell flat on his snout, and nearly flipped the raft. The entire student body went wild then without any encouragement from me.

Shrill as they whistled for more, you might have thought they were a flock of trumpeter swans, not civilized river trolls with thimbles and manners and teacups all waiting at home.

Once everyone had settled down, Savious braced himself as if about to try and lift a mountain. He opened his mouth to say something staggeringly important and pointed a trembling claw at the nearest student.

Not a peep came out though. He stayed locked up that way for a minute or so, turning a throbbing, moldy, lovely shade of green, same as he did every year when calling out the first number.

Mustering all his courage, he finally sputtered, "Seven!"

My students cringed and held their breaths as if expecting tentacles to come boiling out of the river to snatch them.

When all that happened was the surfacing of a mossy snapping turtle with a folded football jersey on its back, everyone exhaled big time.

I waved the nearest student closer and handed out the first purple and gold uniform of the new school year.

"Seven," I repeated after Savious.

For all we knew, the jersey's number said forty-eight, but then again, maybe it didn't. No one present was about to go correcting a rock troll even if they knew he was wrong, which they didn't. Not when it came to numbers, they didn't.

Tomtom pointed at a second student, cleared his throat, and squeaked, "Ninety-nine."

Another turtle surfaced with a folded jersey whose number might have said ninety-nine. Or then again, maybe not. I was in agreement with Tomtom though and passed the jersey out, saying, "Ninety-nine."

When it was Vroom's turn, he needed some coaching from Savious but finally managed to get out a number, though you could tell his palms, armpits, and between his toes were sweating by the time he said it.

"Twelve," he shouted as if goosed.

And so it went. Each student received their school uniform without a single one of them trying to skip out.

If I could get rock trolls to hand out numbers, who knew what else I could do? I counted on my students being worried about that. Another school year had begun.

The Bell

Once everyone had tugged on their uniforms, I lined them up in pairs and dove to the one-room schoolhouse down below. Their desks had been cleaned of nesting perch, and star-grass had been used to scrub the floors. The catfish who lived up in the rafters looked down on us as if we'd never left.

Taking my place at the head of the classroom, I waited until all my students were seated and facing front. Slowly, I scanned up and down the aisles, making eye contact with each student, including the one who winked at me. Given the way my eyes worked separately, it didn't take long. I nodded at each and every one of them, as if we'd both just signed a contract to do our best throughout the year.

Done with that, I straightened my posture even more and announced, "Welcome. We've a great deal to learn this year. A lot of river to cover. But before we get started, I wanted to show you a new addition to our academy."

Reaching up, I grabbed hold of a rope that was hanging above my desk. The students' gaze followed the rope up past a rafter, and still farther up, where it disappeared into the small tower above the school.

"Thanks to a recent graduate," I proudly announced, "this year we have a bell."

That caused a stir.

"Settle down," I said.

Once I had their complete attention, I tugged down on the rope with all my might, sending a clear, lovely clang throughout the slough. I hoped it sounded as though calling them to do things far grander than they'd ever thought possible.

Everyone's eyes popped bigger than turtle eggs and tick-tocked back and forth across the ceiling in time with the swinging of the bell. Several seconds passed before anyone got around to closing their mouths.

"Every time you answer a question right," I told them, "You'll get to ring the bell. I expect to hear a great deal of it this year."

Several students swallowed hard, a few looked faint, one raised her paw to ask a question, and the bell just kept right on ringing.

The End

Acknowledgments

A special thank you to the following people for helping to corral these stories: Helen Kay Stefan, Scott Spoolman, Lee Korthof, Dan Rein, Gloria Larson, and Charles Piepho.

Joseph Helgerson was born and raised along the Mississippi River. Catfish and river trolls were his early pals. During the flood of '51 he had to be evacuated from his home by a leaky rowboat. The first school he attended was a one-room country schoolhouse that overlooked the river near Queens Bluff, Minnesota. Today he keeps an eye on the river as it passes through the twin cities of Minneapolis and St. Paul, where he lives with his family.

Lauren Mortimer was born in Tucson, Arizona, and moved to London when two years old. She's stayed there ever since. She finds that living in the city comes with many advantages, but there are times when she just needs to get closer to the natural world. She's at her most content when sitting somewhere quiet and beautiful, observing. No distractions. Just herself, her pencil, paper. And nature.

Milton Keynes UK
Ingram Content Group UK Ltd.
UKHW022344231024
450133UK00001B/37

9 781949 615036